Purely
ROSIE PEARL

Purely
ROSIE PEARL

PATRICIA A. COCHRANE

Delacorte Press

Published by
Delacorte Press
Bantam Doubleday Dell Publishing Group, Inc.
1540 Broadway
New York, New York 10036

Library of Congress Cataloging-in-Publication Data

Cochrane, Patricia A.
  Purely Rosie Pearl / by Patricia A. Cochrane.
    p.   cm.
  Summary: In 1936 twelve-year-old Rosie Pearl Bush and her family of migrants endure the hardships of the Great Depression as they find work picking fruit in the California Valley.
  ISBN 0-385-32193-7 (hardcover)
  [1. Depressions—1929—Fiction. 2. Migrant workers—Fiction. 3. California—Fiction.] I. Title.
  PZ7.C63973Pu   1996
  [Fic]—dc20   95-22178
                                                                   CIP
                                                                    AC

The text of this book is set in 11-point Times New Roman.

Book design by Julie E. Baker

Manufactured in the United States of America

March 1996

10   9   8   7   6   5   4   3   2   1

BVG

*For Warren, my space-maker,
and Mom, the original Maggie.*

Chapter 1

I'm almost never the first one up in my family. So I was surprised, that last day of traveling, when I woke up and looked around the tent. Maw and Paw and Johnny Keats were still sound asleep in their bedrolls. Paw lay spread-eagled on his back, his lips making gentle little puffs as he breathed. Maw just had the little bit of room left on the far side of their double bedroll. She was on her side with her back to the rest of us and her head tucked partway under her pillow. Johnny Keats, my four-year-old brother, had his hand curled under his chin. His favorite pinecone car peeked out of his curved fingers.

Sunlight was trying to creep in around the tent flap, so I knew it wasn't too early. I threw back my covers and grabbed the same pair of hand-me-down knickers I'd worn yesterday. I topped it off with a long-tailed, faded denim shirt I got from the same brother who outgrew the knickers. We've been following the crops since before Johnny Keats was born. I never wear a dress when we're on the road, or when I'm picking, though I have two my sister, Lily Opal, handed down to me. I wear them to school or on Sundays.

I decided to go get water, then surprise Paw by getting the fire started. The sooner we got on the road, the sooner we'd get to the camp we'd stay at while picking this summer. We were about a week behind our regular time to go to California. Maw hadn't been so well, those last few weeks in Yakima. We'd delayed, hoping she'd get to feeling better.

Now I could hardly wait to see Lily Opal and the rest of my family. It was going to be a great day.

Then I remembered my oldest brother, Walter Scott, wouldn't be in camp to welcome us. I wondered where he was and why we hadn't heard from him yet. I shut my mind to the questions I'd been asking myself all winter. No! This was going to be a good day, a happy day for the Bush family.

But soon's I set foot outside our tent, I knew it wasn't going to be a good day at all.

The lid of the food box was open, and five pounds of corn-meal was spread all over the back of the truck. The empty cloth sack lay on the ground, torn to shreds. "Raccoons," I groaned, my stomach flipping like one of Maw's flapjacks. *Rosie Pearl Bush,* I told myself, *you are in big, big trouble.*

"Mind you don't forget to snap the padlock on the food box after you finish cleaning up, Rosie Pearl," Maw had cautioned last night as she led Johnny Keats off to bed.

"I won't forget, Maw," I'd promised, not looking up. But I had.

I was trying to read an old comic strip I'd found in the camp-ground we'd stayed at the night before. It ain't often I get my hands on something to read, even if it is just *Felix the Cat.* Our campfire had burned low, but Paw said not to put on more wood so close to bedtime. Paw was trying to read part of an April 1936 newspaper I'd found in the same trash heap with Felix. Although the paper was a month old, Paw said we could still learn a lot from it about how the depression was going. Every so often he'd read a headline aloud: "Unemployment Reaches Eighty Percent in Some Cities," "Dispossessed Dust-bowlers Pour into California." Both these headlines were followed by reminders of how lucky we were to have jobs waiting for us.

Then Paw had folded his newspaper, saving it to read again or for some other practical use. That's one thing we're learning to do during this depression: Use it up, wear it out, make do, or do without. And that meant even old newspapers.

I had looked quickly back at my funny paper. I'd hoped I could finish one more page, though by then I could hardly see the pictures, much less the words. That's why my mind hadn't been on what Maw said about locking the food box.

Now, looking at the mess in the back of the truck, I knew my excuse wouldn't cover the loss of a whole sack of cornmeal.

I could almost hear what Maw would say if I tried. "An excuse is like a bucket with a hole in it, Rosie Pearl. No matter how much water you pour in, sooner or later, you're gonna be standing there with an empty bucket!"

How I hate that saying, especially when I know it's true.

I lifted the tent flap a couple of inches and looked back inside. Maw and Johnny Keats still slept soundly, but Paw was beginning to stir. I dropped the flap, wondering what to do first.

Should I clean up the back of the truck, or go for water? I heard Paw stretch and yawn. I wanted to grab the water pail and run. I didn't want to be there when either of my folks came out of that tent.

But that would only be putting off bad for worse, Maw would say. I ran for the back of the truck and climbed up.

Cornmeal crunched under my feet as I searched for the

3

broom. I thought about all the pans of corn bread or stacks of flapjacks Maw could have made from that bag of meal. My stomach flipped with anxiety, but now from hunger, too.

I had all the little yellow bits I could see swept into a pile when Paw stepped out of the tent. He was bent practically in two, being he's so tall. He pulled up his suspenders, then swept his hair back, and put on his cap to hold it in place. Funny about towheaded folks when they go gray. That soft gold color turns to even softer-looking silver.

"Oh, no!" Paw said when he saw the open box and then the pile. The wrinkles on his face deepened, especially those around his mouth. I felt awful all over again. I purely hate disappointing my paw.

"I forgot, Paw," I said quickly. "I'm awful sorry." My voice wavered, and I felt tears come into my eyes. Nervously I scrubbed at them with the back of my hand.

Paw picked his way over the rocky ground in his stocking feet, his old work boots still in his hand. I knew he wouldn't yell at me. Maw would take care of that. Paw can make me feel more ashamed with a few quiet words than all Maw's yelling.

"We all forget sometimes, Rosebud," he said. "But this . . ." The sweep of his hand ended at the empty bag.

I sniffed, and my eyes filled again.

Paw cleared his throat and frowned. He's kind of funny about being around people who are crying. It makes him right uncomfortable. I'm usually that way, too. But lately my eyes seem to tear up easy. Maw says it's because I'm gonna be a teenager next year.

Paw picked up the water pail and held it under the bed of the truck. He nodded toward the broom. I swept the cornmeal into the pail, then jumped down.

He handed me the pail. "Empty this somewheres out of

4

sight," he said. "It might could be the birds'll get some good out of it." He closed the food box, then sat down on a log and started pulling on his boots. "And take your time getting water," he added. "I'll tell your maw what happened. Maybe she'll be calmed down a mite by the time you get back."

"Thanks, Paw." I gave him a quick, relieved hug around his thin neck, then took off down the path to the water tap. I knew Maw would still give me a tongue-lashing, no matter how much Paw softened her up.

A short walk into the bushes took care of the ruined cornmeal. Since the rabies scare last year, Maw won't cook with anything that's been touched by raccoons or squirrels.

I saw the drips from the water tap hitting the ground before I even got to it. Down the path a girl walked away from me, carrying a water pail.

"Some people!" I grumbled as I watched her sashay along in her full-skirted dress. I wished it wasn't so early in the morning. I'd have yelled at her for sure. Easy to see she wasn't no Californian, wasting water that way.

Funny, I thought. That girl sure is dressed fancy for being in a campground. Of course I'd noticed that the campgrounds between Washington and California were somewhat fancier themselves this year. Everyone was commenting on it. Paw said the new trails, picnic tables, fire pits, and outhouses were the work of the boys and young men in the Civilian Conservation Corps. CCC boys, they were called. The CCC was one of President Roosevelt's programs for making jobs where there hadn't been any before.

But that girl still looked out of place to me. The ribbons at the ends of her dark braids matched the leaves on her flowered dress. Neat white socks gleamed over her shiny brown oxfords.

I decided she must come from a rich family. Taking a break

5

on their way to some fancy resort. But bringing along a regular old water pail?

Like Maw says, you meet all kinds on the road these days. One thing for sure, I wouldn't be seeing the likes of her in the Sacramento Valley camp we were headed for.

The girl turned a bend in the path, and I went to wondering what was going on back at our campsite. How was Maw taking the news? Was she working up to holler at me?

One time I had asked Lily Opal why Maw and Paw acted so different when one of us got in trouble. She'd said she thought it had to do with their own growing-up years. Paw was the baby in a family of five boys and six girls. They were flatland farmers in Missouri, and they did right well. "It was like Paw had seven mothers," Lily Opal had explained. "They were all quiet women, and they kept life smooth and protected for him. But don't get the idea he was a sissy," she had gone on. "Paw's quiet, but I ain't never met a stronger man." Lily Opal was right; Paw is a strong man, inside and out.

"Maw's family were farmers, too," Lily Opal had then reminded me. "But their hilly farm in Oklahoma barely grew enough food to keep them through the winter, even though there were only six of them. Maw says every one of them had a mouth on them you could scarce believe. Not only for eating, but trying to outtalk each other. Maw was the oldest of them four kids, and the only girl. She was only eleven when their mother died, and little Edith, our maw, helped her paw raise up her three little brothers."

I remembered hearing Maw tell this part of the story. But what did raising her brothers have to do with how different she was from Paw when I did something bad?

Lily Opal had smiled a crooked smile. "The only way Maw could keep control around that house was to outyell all of them, including her own daddy.

6

"So even now, when one of us do something dumb, Maw forgets she's not raising us alone. Paw reminds her that he's here to help, too."

What a hard life little Edith had, I thought, having my usual hard time seeing Maw and Paw as kids. Not that life's all that easy now, what with this depression going on and on. The roads are full of people from all over the United States, looking for work, any kind of work. And not all the people who end up following the crops know anything about farming. Why, I've picked with shopkeepers and bank tellers and even former teachers. I usually try to keep away from them. Whenever they pick anywhere near a kid, they tend to slip right back into their teacher role.

I set my pail on the wet ground and turned on the tap. How could I have been so careless? I didn't have money to buy another bag of cornmeal now, and neither did Paw. I couldn't even do extra chores to help make up for it. I was already doing most of the cooking and cleaning up, with Maw still not feeling well.

But Maw would see to it that the money would come from my pay when we started picking. Not that every penny we make hasn't already been spent three or four times in our minds. The point would be: Rosie Pearl didn't lock the food box. Rosie Pearl has to earn the money to replace the cornmeal.

Maw had paid two dollars for that sack of meal. All grain products were high these days with so many farms still failing. It was going to take me four full days of picking to earn two dollars, and that's if I really hustled.

I shook my head sadly as water splashed into my pail. Meals would be a little less filling until I got picking money to replace that bag of cornmeal. And it would cost more in the little store near the migrant camp than it had in the big store in Yakima. Probably Paw would wait until he had a chance to get into town,

7

hoping the folks there wouldn't have jacked up their prices for migrants.

Taking Paw at his word, I didn't hurry much after the pail was full. Instead I looked around to see if Betty Mae Perkins and her family might be behind schedule, too. Betty Mae and me had promised to pick with each other this season. I'd thought about that this past winter, too, wondering if it had been a good idea. Betty Mae and me didn't really have much in common, except being girls. She likes to read her mother's *True Romance* magazines, and she sends for all the free samples—like Tangee lipstick, and Pond's Cold Cream. She gave me one of the lipsticks one time. It wasn't her color, she said. I don't know if it's my color, either. I never got up the nerve to try it.

As I looked around now, only the Tates' old, patched-up army tent was familiar. I hurried quick-like past that. Me and Teddy Tate hadn't got along too good last season. I didn't care if I ever saw him again.

Maw was up and dressed when I got back to our campsite, her feed-sack apron tied over her only dress. Once we started picking, she'd just wear it on Sunday, our day off. *Maw must be feeling better if she's thinking about cooking,* I thought, eyeing her big-boned frame curiously. Then she looked up and saw me.

I know Paw must have tried to talk her out of being mad at me. He wouldn't say he'd try and then not do it. But Maw just needs to let off a certain amount of steam every so often. Once she gets it out, she's her regular easygoing self again, and she never holds a grudge.

But Maw is loud, and it's kinda embarrassing if someone out of the family is around. Paw must have reminded her how early it still was. There wasn't hardly anyone else up and around. "Rosie Pearl Bush!" she rasped, right at the top of her whispering voice.

I flinched. Her words seemed to bounce off the sides of the

tents and trees surrounding us. I didn't say a word. I've learned the hard way to keep my mouth shut when Maw's scolding me. If I say even one small "But Maw," she's likely to back up and start all over again.

But this morning it didn't take her long at all. Maybe Paw was getting better at unsteaming her. "There's all kinds of responsibilities, Rosie Pearl. There's the way you been helping out ever since I, since I been feeling poorly." Maw's round face got kind of red. "I'm right proud of you for that."

She shook her head, and her short cropped hair swung over her ears. "But forgetting to lock the food box!"

I opened my mouth to say "I know, Maw. I'll never do it again." Fortunately I caught myself, closed my mouth, and listened.

"What's done's done, Rosie Pearl," she said, her voice just medium loud. "This scolding is over, and I ain't gonna mention it again."

I glanced down at Johnny Keats, playing in the dirt with his pinecones. His eyes were wide and curious.

"Thanks, Maw," I said meekly. Johnny Keats tipped me a solemn wink, his whole face scrinched up with the effort. I turned away so he wouldn't see my smile, but he'd already gone back to his game. I watched him a moment, wishing he had real toy cars to play with.

"Craaash!" he shouted, banging two big cones together at the crossroads he'd scratched in the dirt. "Call an am'blance! Call the po-leece!"

Good thing there's lots of pinecones around.

9

Chapter 2

I was back carrying empty buckets to a water tap that afternoon soon after we got to the migrant camp in the Sacramento Valley where we were going to pick. There's nothing special about the valley, but it is big. Only Lily Opal had been there to welcome us; the others were off in the fields, picking. I was so glad to see Lily Opal, I didn't mind waiting to see them.

Not that I got to talk to her. Maw asked most of the questions I'd wanted to ask, so Paw and I sat and listened. Sometimes I can be like Paw.

"Just look what Buddy made," Lily Opal squeezed between two of Maw's questions. She patted the arms of the rocking chair she sat in. "He started it the day after we found out about our baby."

"Buddy's our number one son-in-law," Maw said proudly.

Lily Opal giggled. "He's your only son-in-law, Maw." She winked at me. "At least, until Rosie Pearl gets married."

"Mercy!" Maw shouted. "Don't even talk about things like that. Rosie Pearl's only twelve. She's still a little girl!"

Lily Opal giggled again as I rolled my eyes.

Maw leaned forward and lowered her voice. "So, how do you like your new sister-in-law?"

Robbie Burns, the youngest of my two older brothers, had got himself married during the winter.

"You're gonna like her, Maw," Lily Opal said. "She's quiet, like Paw, and a good cook, like you."

I picked at a dried spot of food on my knickers. I'm not real good around quiet people, until I get to know them. It's so hard to tell what quiet people are thinking.

But I liked the idea of another good cook in the family, especially if Maw started feeling poorly again.

"We saved a cabin for you, Maw," Lily Opal said through a wide yawn. "It's right next door. Buddy and Robbie Burns swept it out and got it ready."

Maw got up. "Humph, we'll see what them two know about cleaning a cabin." She pointed at me. "Water, Rosie Pearl. Your sister needs a nap, and we need water to clean our cabin."

I got up, too, sighing. I knew that "we" meant Maw and me.

"Johnny Keats and me will unload the truck," Paw said to Maw as he dropped a kiss on the top of Lily Opal's head. "We'll just pile things on the porch until you're ready for them, Edith."

Finally the cabin was clean to Maw's satisfaction. Everything was done, except filling the mattress ticks. Maw sat down on a stool. "I'm too tired to wait for a mattress," Maw said. "Just pile them quilts on the bottom bunks, Orrin, so Johnny Keats and me can have our naps."

I edged for the door. "Fill the pail again, Rosie Pearl," Maw said. "And see if Lily Opal needs water, too. Then you can play. I'll call if I need you."

I grabbed our pail and went next door. Lily Opal was still

napping, but her empty pail was by the door. I grabbed it, too, and took off at a trot. This water was for after-supper dishes. I had at least an hour to myself, maybe two if Maw didn't need me.

I moved kinda fast around the corner of our cabin row, then saw something that stopped me still in my tracks.

It was that girl again! The one in the dress and matching hair ribbons. She stood, leaning back against the cabin row while water poured over the sides of her full pail. This time I'd tell her what I'd wanted to just that morning.

"Hey, stupid!" I shouted. "Shut off that tap. Can't you see you're wasting water and getting the ground all muddy?"

I reckon she hadn't heard me coming. She jerked upright, and her foot hit a patch of mud. It slid right out from under her. She fell hard, right on her rear end. Her flowered skirt flipped up, and I saw lace on her underpants.

I started to chant, "I see London, I see France . . . ," then stopped, maybe because I wasn't wearing lacy underwear. I wasn't wearing *any* underwear. Maw hadn't paid much mind to things like washing clothes since we'd left Yakima four days earlier.

The trouble is, when we're traveling, I don't think about things like clean underwear until I'm in my bedroll at night. When you're sleeping in a five-by-nine tent with three other people, you can't get up and rummage around after everyone's settled in.

So I didn't finish what I was yelling, but that girl glared at me like I had. A body would think I was the one doing something dumb, not her.

She scrambled up and smoothed down her skirt before reaching to turn off the water tap. "It'll dry out fast enough," she said in a low voice. "It's so hot it's a wonder this whole valley doesn't dry up and blow away." One corner of her mouth was turned up, looking halfway between a sneer and a smile.

I know about land blowing away. It's one subject we don't talk about in my family. Our farm was right in the middle of the Dust Bowl. It wasn't the farm Paw grew up on; his oldest brother got that. But it was a good farm, until the years of drought when the wind came and blew away all the topsoil. No one can farm land, no matter how good it once was, without good soil, and rain, and as few bugs as possible. Our farm didn't have any of those things by the time we drove away that last day.

The whole Bush family is following the crops these days because we lost the farm.

"Oh, yeah?" I told that girl, kicking loose dirt over the muddy spots. "That's all you know about it. This valley is irrigated. It isn't going to blow away."

She shrugged. "Wouldn't hurt my feelings any if it did. I didn't want to come to this awful place anyway. This must be the worst place in the world."

I glanced around. She was right. A California pickers' camp is an awful place on a hot summer afternoon. Dirt, dead grass clumps, and pathetic stands of dusty-leaved trees are all that meet the eye from the porches of row after row of cramped, back-to-back, one-room cabins. The water tap at one end of each row and outhouse at the other don't add much to the scenery, either.

Beyond the camp, the valley stretches for miles to the surrounding mountains. Lots of it is planted fields and orchards, but they're not much to look at when you've just spent the whole day picking in another field or orchard.

The only good thing I could say about the camp right then was that it was quiet. Most everybody was out in the fields, picking. But when the picking day ended, that whole place would

13

fill up with dirty, tired, and hungry people. Noisiest of all were the little kids like Johnny Keats who were too little to pick. They'd have been under some grown-up's watchful eye all day long as they played at the edge of a field, or toted water, or napped.

So when they got back to camp, they stayed outside, running and yelling. And most of them were cranky. I knew; I was in charge of Johnny Keats while Maw made supper.

Sometimes it wasn't any quieter in the cabins. Men yelled at their wives to keep the kids quiet. Wives yelled back that they had enough to do to get the supper on the table.

But it was the after-supper, after-dark yelling I dreaded most. That was when the home brew came out. It was when men started remembering good jobs they'd once had. And even though I'd told her none of this, over her dark eyes the girl's eyebrows rose slowly, as if to say "See what I mean about this place? A little water on the ground isn't going to make it look any worse."

I tightened my jaw, feeling my dander start to rise. I don't know what gets into me sometimes. It's like my mouth works faster than my brain.

"If you hate it so much, why don't you just get out of here?" I asked, trying to match my tone to hers.

"Maybe I will," she replied, her voice still calm and even. "My father's looking for someone to tell him where to sign up for picking. If I'm lucky, there won't be anyplace for us to pick around here."

I tried out a smiling sneer of my own. "Well, I'll tell you one thing," I said. "If the rest of your family all dress like you do, your luck will probably hold. Jake Porter don't hire no fancy pants."

Now it was her turn to say something. But she didn't. She stared at me, that one corner of her mouth still turned up.

14

I'm really patient, especially in staring contests. I propped myself against the building and waited. Holding my eyes wide open so I wouldn't blink, I moved slowly back and forth, scratching my back against the rough, whitewashed boards.

Pretty soon I begun to feel a mite uneasy. That girl sure knew how to stare!

That morning I'd noticed she was about my age, and how neat and tidy she looked. But those things hadn't meant anything to me. I hadn't expected to ever see her again.

Now I glanced down at my big sloppy shirt and the holes in the knees of my knickers. I was as far from neat and tidy as a body could be.

She stared all the way down me and back up again. Her nose wrinkled slightly when she got to my dirty feet.

She stared at my knickers, and I wondered if my legs were dirty, too, showing through the holes in the knees. I reached for my belt to hitch up my knickers and close the gap between them and my shirt. But she looked, quick-like, at my hands so I stuffed them in my pockets.

All the while she stared she was fooling with the green taffeta ribbon on one of her long, dark braids. The darkest red—Maw calls that color auburn. I'd like hair that color. It's nothing special being a blue-eyed towhead in my family.

She shrugged. "I'd rather be called fancy pants than go around looking like a tramp."

"Hold on there!" I hollered. "Who you calling a tramp?" I flung down my empty pails and started toward her.

She grabbed her pail. When I got about four steps from her, quick as a grasshopper, she tipped some of the water toward me and skedaddled around the corner of the cabin row.

The water sloshed right under my feet, and I flopped down into the instant mud. I came up spitting mad, my knickers so wet and muddy they almost fell down.

By the time I got my pants hitched up, she was out of sight. I took off after her anyway. Nobody gets away with saying I look like a tramp.

It didn't take long to catch up. She'd only run down the next row of cabins, then around to the shady side. Her back was to me, and I slowed down as I got closer. *That must be her maw,* I thought, spotting a woman sitting on a camp stool. She was all dressed up, too. Then I saw that, fresh ironed as their clothes were, they were far from new. The girl's skirt had been let down more than once, and someone had used Maw's trick of putting rickrack over the old hem lines.

"Is this enough water, Mama?" the girl was asking. "There was a strange-looking person at the water tap, and I spilled some, hurrying to get away."

"Who you calling strange-looking?" I demanded, stumbling to a halt.

The girl turned and stared at me. This was the staringest girl I had ever seen! But I'd seen this look before. It said: "You're gonna get it now!"

So I tossed back a look that said: "Not without a fight, I ain't!"

"I don't suppose that kid told you she's been name-calling," I asked the woman angrily.

She looked surprised. "Oh, I'm sure you must be mistaken."

Oh, great! One of those parents who think their kids can do no wrong. Most folks who follow the crops let their kids settle their own fights.

I shook my head, forgetting I'd ever had manners. "She was name-calling all right!"

"Margaret," the woman said calmly. "What is going on?"

"Maggie," the girl said softly, glancing briefly away from me.

Her maw frowned. "Don't tell *me* what to call you, young lady. I named you."

"But everyone else calls me Maggie."

"Never mind everyone else. And don't change the subject."

I grinned. Maybe I was wrong about this woman.

"And what's *your* name, young lady?" the woman asked me.

"Rosie Pearl," I said. "Rosie Pearl Bush."

Margaret snickered. But when her maw frowned again, she quit snickering right fast.

"I'm Nellie Campbell," the woman said. "And this is my daughter, whose name, as you heard, is Margaret."

I nodded briefly. This wasn't a social call.

"I'd just as soon she didn't call me anything," Margaret muttered.

I snickered back. Letting another kid find out you don't like your name is the fastest way to be sure that's exactly what they'll call you.

Truth to tell, with that dark red hair she looked more like a Maggie than a Margaret. *But if she sticks around here,* I thought, *I'm gonna call her Margaret.*

Chapter 3

"I'd like an answer, Margaret," Mrs. Campbell said. "Did you insult Rosie Pearl?"

"I might have."

"Come now, what did you say?"

Margaret looked down at her feet. "I said maybe we wouldn't be staying here," she mumbled.

"Liar!" I shouted. "That's not what I'm talking about."

"Now, now," Mrs. Campbell cautioned. "Calling names never solved anything."

"But she *is* lying! She said I looked like a tramp."

"Margaret Grace Campbell! Is that true?" Mrs. Campbell cried, jumping to her feet.

"Close enough," Margaret said.

As Mrs. Campbell tilted her head to look up into my face, I realized how tiny she was. Why, she'd only come up to Maw's shoulder, and way below Paw's. Her soft, wavy hair framed her face—like Maw's used to after she'd rolled it up in rags at night.

Her hair was reddish, too, but only a shade or so darker than mine.

"Rosie Pearl," she said, making a steeple of her fingers and tapping her chin. "Will you sit down and talk this out with Margaret?"

"If I do, are you gonna hit her afterwards?" I asked.

Mrs. Campbell shook her head slowly. "No, I don't hit my child." She paused. "Though some parents do." She raised her eyebrows questioningly.

"Not mine," I said quickly. "Oh, Maw hands out a swat now and again, when I do some dumb little thing. But when I get in big trouble, Paw talks at me about it. Sometimes I'd rather he did hit me."

Mrs. Campbell chuckled. "I know the feeling. I had a father like that, too."

Curious to know what would happen, I said, "Reckon I could stay for a bit."

"Good!" Mrs. Campbell beamed at me. "Margaret, get a stool for our guest."

"No, thank you, ma'am," I said. I plopped myself down on a patch of dried grass. "My knickers are too muddy for nice stools."

"I noticed that," Mrs. Campbell said with a slight frown. "And you've mud on your clean dress, Margaret. Perhaps we'll have to get you knickerbockers, like Rosie Pearl's."

"Mama!" Margaret gasped. "Surely you don't expect me to wear boy's pants."

"Well," her mother replied, "you know the old saying, 'When in Rome, do as the Romans do.' In a pickers' camp, folks dress like pickers."

Margaret's mouth was hanging slightly open. Mrs. Campbell stood up and reached for the almost-empty pail. "I need to stretch my legs, and I do need a bit more water than this. When I get back I expect you girls to have your differences all ironed out.''

When Mrs. Campbell was out of hearing, Margaret said, ''Too bad my papa's not here. He'd say, 'There goes my Maggie, getting her dander up again.' ''

Hey, she's spunky, too, I thought. *Good thing I'm not looking to be friends. We'd rub each other the wrong way every time we opened our mouths.*

''And there's no need for you to hang around,'' she added. ''I'm not going to make up with you, and my mother's not going to hit me!'' With that she swiveled around on her stool until her back was to me.

''We'll see about that, Margaret Grace,'' I said. ''We'll just see!'' I spun around on my clump of grass so my back was toward hers.

And we sat that way until her mother returned.

As she got back with her pail of water, Mr. Campbell arrived from the other direction. He was bareheaded, and I knew for sure now where Margaret got her auburn hair.

Then I looked to see how he was dressed. It had been a long time since I'd seen a man wearing a suit. His was an out-of-style one with slightly frayed cuffs. ''Maggie, what's your mother doing carrying water?'' he asked. ''You were supposed to do that for her.''

''It's all right, Ed,'' Mrs. Campbell said. ''Margaret got water for me. But I needed more, and I also needed to stretch my legs.''

''Okay,'' he said, switching to a smile. ''But you rest here while Maggie and I go see the job boss, Nellie. You aren't used to so much traveling.''

Mrs. Campbell grinned at me. ''Married fifteen years, and he still thinks I'm delicate, just because I'm tiny.''

That's when Mr. Campbell spotted me. "Who's this, Maggie? A new friend?"

"Not likely," I said, getting to my feet. "I've got to get back to our cabin. My maw's been feeling poorly lately."

"I'm sorry to hear that," Mrs. Campbell said. "Has she been sick long, Rosie Pearl?"

"Coupla weeks," I said. "I don't think she's too sick. Likely she's carrying again."

"Carrying what?" Margaret asked.

"Land o' Goshen, Margaret Grace!" I burst out. "Don't you know nothing?"

Margaret started to answer me back, but Mrs. Campbell spoke up quick-like. "Rosie Pearl thinks her mother might be pregnant."

"Why didn't she just say so?"

"I did," I said indignantly. I hesitated. "Maw don't like for me to use that word."

"You mean *pregnant*?" Margaret asked. "It's the proper word, isn't it, Mama? It's the word your college book used."

College? I looked at Mrs. Campbell with new interest. What was she doing in a migrant camp? The depression again, I suppose.

"Strange," Margaret mused. "Strange not to use the right word."

I lifted my chin and stepped forward.

But Mrs. Campbell eased between us. "Not strange," she said lightly. "Just different. Every family has its own way of saying things."

She gave my shoulder a little squeeze. "And if we pick at the same places, you girls could learn many new things from each other before the summer is over."

Well! I better not learn to say pregnant, I thought. *Maw would skin me alive!*

21

* * *

$\mathcal{I}$ raced back to the water tap. After filling my pails I sloshed, quick-like, back to our cabin. I sure hoped Paw hadn't gone to check in with Jake Porter, the job boss. Even though Paw had signed up last fall to pick again this summer, I knew he was a bit worried about getting here late. But likely Jake had held our jobs. He knew hiring the best made him look good with the growers, and us Bushes were some of the best.

Usually I stayed away from Jake. But I wanted to be there when he turned Margaret and her family down. Then Margaret would have to leave, and I would never have to see that lopsided smile again.

Paw was just climbing into the truck when I got to our cabin row. "Wait for me, Paw," I called. "I want to go with you."

I set one pail by our doorway and stuck my head into our cabin. Maw and Johnny Keats were in their bunks, sound asleep. I tiptoed next door where my sister, Lily Opal, was rocking in her chair again. "Here's water, Sis." I put the second bucket down.

Lily Opal grinned. "I've been waiting for you to come back so's we could have a good old gab-fest."

I felt a quick twinge of guilt. There's nobody in the world I love more than my sister. I'd about been going crazy to see her ever since she'd written to tell us she was going to have a baby next fall. But we had all summer to talk. Now I really wanted to go with Paw and see what happened to snooty Margaret and her father!

"Well, uhm, Paw's waiting for me to go with him to see the job boss."

Lily Opal looked surprised. "How come you want to go there?" she asked. "You can't stand the sight of Jake Porter."

"In case the growers got smart this winter and fired him," I said.

22

"They didn't. We been here a week, and he's hanging around the fields every day."

I shrugged. "Guess I'll go anyway and keep Paw company."

"Okay," she said, pulling herself to her feet and heading for her bunk again. "I'll rest some more, and we'll talk after supper."

I frowned as I ran to the truck. Lily Opal sure was resting a lot.

I climbed into the front seat next to Paw. We didn't talk much as we drove. *Is he still worried about our jobs?* I wondered. I felt uneasy about something myself. Did I really believe I'd feel good if Jake didn't give the Campbells jobs? *Sure you will,* a little voice said. *Didn't Margaret start all this by saying you looked like a tramp?*

Hoo, boy, Rosie Pearl, I thought, *you're the one oughta be back in camp taking a nap. You're so tired you're talking to yourself. And you've just about convinced yourself you'd rather see Jake Porter browbeat another poor migrant than give jobs to his family.*

I wriggled back into the corner of the seat and shut my eyes. It had sure enough been a long and tiring trip.

The tiring part had started four days earlier, on that last morning in Washington. I had pushed bundles and boxes around in the back of the truck, fixing up a place to ride. I was looking forward to the time alone.

Johnny Keats came running out of the cabin. "Paw says I'm big enough to ride with you this year." He jumped up and down. "C'mon, Rosie Pearl, I gotta fix me a nest, too!"

I stared at him. Paw kidded *me* about being his chick-a-biddy hen, making myself a nest. Now I had to make room for another? Paw came out of the cabin, and Johnny Keats held up his arms. "Lift me up, Paw, lift me up."

23

"First run see if Maw has anything more for you to carry out," Paw said.

I groaned, knowing what was coming next.

We'd wintered over for the past three years at this apple ranch near Yakima. Our one-room cabin was pretty much like those in the migrant camps in California, as small and crowded as the classrooms in the public schools I go to for a few months every winter.

Maw and me had looked that cabin over real careful. There wasn't a thing left to carry out. Paw just wanted to talk to me alone.

"Rosebud," Paw said hesitantly as Johnny Keats ran off. "You know your maw ain't feeling too well lately?"

"Yeah, I know." We'd put off leaving for California past our usual time, hoping Maw would get over whatever was bothering her.

"We can't put off leaving no longer," Paw went on. "If we do, Jake Porter might have to give our jobs to someone else."

"Yeah," I said again. When fruit and vegetables are ready to be picked, there's no waiting.

"Maw'd sure be a whole lot more comfortable without Johnny Keats climbing all over her." Paw had a question in his voice. That meant I had to decide.

As usual, Paw was talking sense. The cab of our truck is small, but there's plenty of room in back, now my older sister and brothers don't travel with us anymore.

I swallowed a sigh. "Sure, Paw," I said. "I reckon Johnny Keats will fall to sleep right after lunch anyway."

And he had. All four days of the trip. But I was still worn out every night when we finally stopped at a campground. We were all worn out, especially Paw. Seems like every time we rounded a curve, there was another crew working on the road. "Ooops,"

Paw shouted one day, hitting the brakes. "Here's some more WPA workers."

"What's double-you-pea-ay, Paw?" I heard Johnny Keats ask.

"That's the Works Progress Administration," Paw answered. "Another of President Roosevelt's plans to make more jobs. But I wish to heaven they were workin' somewheres else and not slowin' me down like this."

Ever since this depression started several years back, Paw's been saying how lucky we are that the growers want our family to come back every spring. "Anyone with any kinda job is lucky these days," he says.

Each night, after I helped Paw get the tent up, I grabbed the water pail and looked as I walked to see if any other pickers were stopping at this campground for the night.

Each night, soon as the tent was up, Maw went in to take a rest. I was in charge of getting supper started and helping Paw look after Johnny Keats. It's times like these I miss my older sister and brothers most. I'm stuck with being the oldest now.

Chapter 4

The truck hit a pothole, and I opened my eyes. We were almost to Jake Porter's shack.

I yawned, thinking Maw and Lily Opal were the smart ones. Though I hated to admit it, I was tired enough for a nap, too. No wonder I'd reared back and hollered at Margaret!

Maw gets upset when I talk first and think later. "Listen here, missy!" she said to me one time. "One of these days you're gonna say something that'll make you wish you hadn't never learned to talk at all."

Imagine wishing you couldn't talk! Just thinking about it made me extra careful for about a month. Then again, knowing me, maybe it was only a few days.

When we pulled up at Jake Porter's shack, another car was already parked there. As I followed Paw I heard Jake shouting. "Who do yew think yew are, comin' in here all dressed up in a suit and tie and makin' me think yew was a grower?

"Nobody works 'round here 'lesn I sez so!" Jake hollered.

He was getting louder with every word. "Any openings I has is fer my regulars."

I was still right behind Paw when Margaret Campbell came rushing out the door.

"Oh, it's you," she said, stiffening when she saw me. She gestured back through the door. "That man is like everything else in this place. Awful! He won't let my father get a word in edgewise."

"I thought you didn't want him to give you jobs, Margaret. I thought you wanted to get outta here," I said, keeping my voice calm, since Paw was watching.

Her face turned red, and she looked at her feet. "Well, yes but . . . ," she mumbled. "We *have* to get work. And these are the only jobs around." Her face looked blotchy, like she was ready to burst out crying.

Paw must have noticed, too. "You know each other, Rose-bud?" he asked quickly.

I nodded. "We met back at camp, Paw. But Margaret and her folks ain't staying there. They don't have jobs yet."

Paw looked inside. Jake Porter had stopped yelling. He had turned his back on Mr. Campbell, waiting for him to leave.

Jake's office is real small. There's not room for more than a desk and a chair, and one or two people. The rest of the place is his living quarters, but the door to it is always shut.

"Stay outta the way, girls," Paw said. "I'll take care of this."

Quick-like, I decided that *outta the way* didn't mean off the porch. Margaret scooted next to me. I pressed my nose against the window a second before she did. A moment later Jake Porter turned and saw Paw.

"Whadda yew want, Bush?" he shouted.

"No call for you to use that tone with me, Jake," Paw said

quietly. "Or to an honest request for a job, when there's spaces empty."

Paw turned to Mr. Campbell. "My name's Orrin Bush. You looking for work?"

Mr. Campbell held out his hand. "I'm Ed Campbell. Yes, my family needs work."

"Well, yew ain't gonna find any here," Jake yelled across the desk. "I already done told yew twice that there ain't no room for yew."

"I see a coupla empty spaces," Paw said, pointing to Jake's chart.

Porter turned red. "Yew callin' me a liar, Orrin Bush?" For a second his face reminded me of a fox, peeking around a tree at a barking dog, and he said, "Since yer late showin' up, mebbe I should give him yer place!"

"Don't threaten me, Jake. You know the growers would be unhappy if my family didn't pick this season."

Jake scurried out from behind his desk. "Who's threatenin' who now?" he asked. "I'm still the one who sez who works 'round here, and I sez there ain't no space."

"Ooooh," Margaret moaned in my ear. "What are we going to do? We don't have enough money to get back to Seattle. And there are no jobs there anyway."

"Be quiet," I cautioned. "My paw ain't through yet."

Paw's shoulders rose and dropped as he took in a deep breath, then let it go. "It'd be a shame if you had to tell the valley owners there wouldn't be any Bushes picking for them this season."

"Yew can't do that," Porter screamed. "I promised yew'd all show up!"

"Well then," Paw said.

Porter glared at Paw, then grabbed a pencil from the desk. Jaw clenched, he scribbled in "Campbell" on the chart.

Paw turned and walked out of the cabin. Mr. Campbell followed, his mouth hanging slightly open.

Margaret and me followed them off the porch. When we got back out by our truck, Paw sagged against the front fender. "Whew," he said.

Margaret's father gripped Paw's shoulder. "Why did you do that, Mr. Bush? You put your own job in danger."

Paw nodded. "I know. Wondered myself who was talking." He stood up and pulled a clean rag from his hip pocket. "Had to happen, sooner or later," he said, wiping his forehead and neck. "Jake's a hard man to work with, though he does get the job done. But he's a weak man. I was counting pretty heavy on his backing down."

Paw stuffed the rag back in his pocket. "Follow me back to camp, Ed," he said. "We'll find a cabin for you."

I glanced back and saw Jake Porter staring after my paw. A look of pure hate filled his eyes.

Back at the pickers' camp, Johnny Keats came racing out of our cabin as our truck and the Campbells' car pulled up. Maw was close behind him.

I shook my head, knowing what was going to happen next. Maw would make friends with Mrs. Campbell, and she'd expect me to be friends with Margaret, too.

Sure enough, when Mr. Campbell brought his wife to our cabin, the two women took to each other instantly. While Paw went with Mr. Campbell to help him find an empty cabin, Maw and Mrs. Campbell sat down on the edge of the porch and started talking.

And I started listening. They were using different words, but they were talking about the same things: the trip down, how hot it was, how dusty the camp was, and the work of getting settled.

Still feeling grouchy about the way things had turned out, I glanced at Margaret. Right away I felt better. I could have been looking in a mirror at my own grouchy face.

Then Maw got one of her bright ideas. "Rosie Pearl, you and Margaret best get started stuffing mattress ticks. Me and Nellie can't make up the beds until them mattresses is ready."

"Sounds logical to me," Mrs. Campbell said.

My own maw had betrayed me! I beckoned Margaret after me with a jerk of my head.

I led Margaret to the end of the row where a pile of empty blue-striped mattress ticks were stacked next to a pile of dried cornhusks. "Ever stuff a tick?" I asked.

She shook her head.

"Thought so," I muttered. "Well, you do it like this." I picked up the top tick—a big cloth bag, the size of a cabin bunk —and shook it open with one hand. With the other hand I grabbed a fistful of husks. Before shoving them into the tick, I gave the husks a good shake.

"Keep doing this," I explained, reaching for another fistful, "until the tick's chock-full. Skimp, and you'll find out right quick how hard them bunk boards are."

Margaret picked up a tick, shook it open, and reached toward the pile. Halfway there, her hand stopped. "Why do you shake this stuff?" she asked softly.

"To get rid of bugs and mice, silly."

"That's what I was afraid of." She shuddered, then picked up one husk. She looked it over carefully before dropping it into her tick and reaching for another.

"You'll be here all summer at that rate," I cried. "Besides, what's a coupla bugs or a little old mouse? The first time you lay down on that mattress, you'll squash them dead."

She grabbed her stomach and pretended to gag. "Yuck, how do you stand it?"

I didn't know whether to laugh or holler at her. She was acting uppity again, but it was kind of funny. I had felt the same way the first time I had to stuff a tick. Well, I wasn't about to tell her that. Before I could laugh or holler, Lily Opal came around the corner, carrying a stool. She put it near the pile of husks and sat down.

"Thought you ladies might could use some help," she said, ending up with one of her famous Bush family giggles.

I hadn't realized how lonesome I'd been for that giggle. "We sure could use your help," I said. "This is Margaret's first mattress-stuffing party, and she don't rightly know how to act."

"Party?" Margaret squeaked. "Funny kind of party, if you ask me."

I swallowed hard. "You'll see," I said. "Lily Opal can make a party outta most any occasion."

Lily Opal looked up at Margaret. "What's the matter, honey? Too tired to have some fun?"

"I'm okay," Margaret replied sullenly. "I just don't see any fun in shaking bugs and mice out of cornhusks."

"You're right," Lily Opal agreed. "That's why me and Rosie Pearl like to pretend we're doing something else. Like this."

She reached into the pile and, grabbing a big handful of husks, began to sing:

> *"Pickin' up pawpaws,"* (Shake, shake.)
> *"Put 'em in your pocket,"* (Into the tick.)
> *"Pickin' up pawpaws,"* (Shake, shake.)
> *"Put 'em in your pocket. . . ."*

By the third "Pickin' up pawpaws," Margaret reached for the pile, and next thing I knew, the three of us were singing at the top of our lungs and stuffing those ticks fast as we could go.

But when we were done and had returned to pick up our last

mattress, Margaret and me got quiet again. "I'd better go help my mother," Margaret said, and off she went. I helped Lily Opal get up, ignoring the strange way she was looking at me. "Think I'll give that rocking chair another try before Buddy gets home for supper," she said, walking slowly down the porch to her cabin.

Gosh, she looks tired, I thought. *She only picks for a few hours these days. And she looks awful thin for someone who's expecting a baby.*

I was getting excited about Robbie Burns and Mavis and Buddy getting home from the fields. Even though I was a tad nervous about meeting my new sister-in-law, I was looking forward to a wallopaloozer of a reunion that night.

Then I remembered Walter Scott again. At the end of last season Walter Scott had accused Paw of not trying hard enough to keep our farm. Maw told me later that it wasn't really my brother talking. It was the whiskey he had been drinking with the oldest Tate boy. Whoever had done the talking, Walter Scott wasn't with our family this season. Nobody knew where he was.

Chapter 5

Things got noisy in our cabin after Robbie Burns and Mavis and Buddy got home from the fields. Lily Opal came in, stretching and yawning, when she heard all the ruckus.

I kinda stood back while Robbie Burns introduced Mavis to Maw and Paw. Then I reminded myself that Mavis wasn't a stranger. She was family now.

Mavis met me coming around the table. She put her arms around me. Her long, brown hair swished against my cheek. "I've always wanted a sister and a little brother," she whispered in my ear. "I'm so glad the rest of the family is willing to share you."

I felt a little shiver of happiness travel up my back. I liked her already.

We all ate supper together that night. We don't do that often, but everyone wanted to be together. Nobody mentioned Walter Scott. I wondered if I was the only one who missed him when I saw Maw look around the room, then walk quickly to the old cast-iron cookstove. She lifted the corner of her apron and wiped her eyes.

After the supper dishes were cleaned up, I went out to look for Betty Mae again. I heard a bunch of kids playing kick the can over on the far side of camp, but I was too tired to walk that far. I checked out our cabin row and was starting on the next row when someone stepped up behind me and put a pair of grubby hands over my eyes.

Quick-like, I felt behind me with my heel. When I bumped something, I stomped down real hard. That's a trick Robbie Burns taught me. Even when I'm barefooted I can stomp real good. And tonight I was wearing shoes. Even if they did have cardboard inside to cover the holes in the bottoms, I got in a real good stomp.

The hands dropped away, and a familiar voice hollered. It was Teddy Tate. "Aw, gee, Rosie Pearl!" he shouted. "What'd you go and do that for?" He hopped around on one foot, holding on to the other.

I turned and started off in the other direction.

"Hey, now," Teddy sputtered. "That's no way to treat your boyfriend you ain't seen since last fall."

I spun around. Teddy would have hopped right into me if I hadn't held him back with my fist. "You listen to me good, Teddy Tate. You ain't my boyfriend! We usta be good friends, but we ain't friends no more."

I gave him a shove. "And don't talk to me lessen I talk to you first! Got that?"

Teddy's face got flame red. Teddy's got fair skin that burns real easy and the color hair that sometimes gets a kid called Carrot-top. But he's also the kinda boy who won't let nobody call him that.

"Aw, Rosie . . ."

I shoved my fist right up under his nose. "Got it?" I repeated.

"Got it," Teddy mouthed silently, throwing his hands up as if I was gonna hit him.

I thought I heard someone behind me, stifling a giggle, but I wanted to make sure Teddy got my message.

Whoever it was, they had to be reacting to the way Teddy was bobbing around like a prizefighter, protecting his face and pretending to take an occasional blow to the stomach. Teddy can be so funny. Nobody but me knows how sorry I am he started this boyfriend stuff.

Teddy kept watching my face. I knew he was hoping I'd give in and be friends. That's what I'd always done before. But I was still too embarrassed from all the teasing I'd taken on his account last fall.

I planted my feet firmly in the dirt. Hands on my hips, I shoved my face close to his. *"Scram!"* I growled through clenched teeth.

Teddy shrugged and scrammed. I sat down on the nearest porch, my shaking hands held tightly in my lap.

"Well, that was something," said a voice from the far end of the porch. "Bet there's an interesting story behind it."

Oh drat, it was Margaret Campbell!

I took a couple of deep breaths to calm myself. "Not really," I said casually. "Not that I'd tell you, if there was."

I expected a quick comeback; instead I got silence. I must have sat there a full minute. Then I heard a sniffle. I stood up. If she was going to puddle up again, like she had at Jake Porter's place, I was leaving.

But her voice sounded okay when she asked softly, "Why do you hate me?"

Hate her? That stopped me. "But—but," I stammered, "I don't hate you."

"Well," she went on, "then you don't like me very much."

"Hey, Margaret," I said, folding my arms across my chest. "I don't know you well enough to like you or not like you."

She laughed and walked down the porch toward me. "Right you are, Rosebud!" She plopped down on the porch. "So how about giving me a chance?"

I was so tired, I leaned back against a post. "Guess that's only fair," I mumbled. "And by the way, Margaret, my name is Rosie Pearl."

She was grinning like a cat with cream on its whiskers. "And mine is Maggie."

She smoothed her skirt and leaned back against the other post. "So, who's your cute boyfriend?"

I gritted my teeth at the trick she'd played on me. "That's Teddy Tate," I growled. "And he's no friend of mine at all."

"Why not?" she protested. "He seems nice, and he's awfully funny."

"He is nice, and he is funny," I muttered. "But he ain't my boyfriend."

Margaret leaned forward. "Can't you and he just be regular friends?" she asked seriously.

"No! You don't know Teddy like I do. He ain't satisfied with just being friends, and I ain't ready to be nobody's girlfriend, yet."

She shrugged. "I can't see any harm in being friendly."

"Go ahead," I challenged. "Just remember who told you it wouldn't work."

"I will," she said.

Neither of us said anything for almost a full minute.

"So, how old are you?" she asked abruptly.

"Twelve. How about you?"

36

"Eleven and three-quarters," she said. "Maybe when I'm twelve my parents will stop treating me like a little kid."

"Don't count on it," I warned her. "I've got two older brothers, an older sister, *and* my parents. They all still treat me like a kid."

"Same here," Margaret said. "I'm always old enough to do what they want me to do but too young to do what I want to do."

"Same here," I said, slipping my hand over my mouth to cover a yawn.

"How many kids did you say you have in your family?" she asked.

"There's five of us, so far." Would she start teasing me again about not liking to say *pregnant*?

"Wow!" she said. "You're lucky not to be an only child like me. I get all the attention, whether I want it or not. So, where do all of them live?"

"Wherever there's crops to pick, like us."

"Oh," Maggie said. "They're migrants, too?"

I'd just started to ask her what was wrong with that when I heard Maw shouting for me. And right on top of that I heard Mrs. Campbell calling, "Margaret!"

For once I was glad to hear Maw shouting. I'd had enough of Margaret—I mean, Maggie—for one day.

"G'night," I mumbled, heading for home. "Maybe I'll see you tomorrow."

In the morning Paw said he'd told the Campbells they could ride to the fields with us. There was room for both families in our truck, and the two men could share the cost of the gas.

That wasn't the only bad news at breakfast. "Rosie Pearl," Maw said firmly. "I want you to pick with Margaret today. She's new, and she'll need to be shown how."

"Good morning!" Maggie said cheerfully as we climbed up into the back of the truck. I just nodded. I don't usually feel much like talking first thing in the morning. I leaned back against the cab of the truck and shut my eyes.

When we got to the fields, Paw said to Mrs. Campbell, "Edith'll tell you how things work 'round here." Then he winked at Maw. "Don't talk her arm off, Edith. She'll need it for picking."

Maw punched him on the shoulder, and we watched as he walked off with Mr. Campbell to check in with the field foreman.

I felt a little jealous that Paw hadn't asked me to go with him. Me being the oldest at home these days, Paw and me had spent a lot of time together lately. To get my mind off that, I started searching the fields for Betty Mae Perkins.

Maw chuckled as the men got past hearing distance. "I'm an awful talker," she admitted. "But that man of mine's so quiet, I talk to m'self sometimes, just for company."

"Company?" Mrs. Campbell sounded surprised. "But Margaret tells me you have five children."

"Yes, but the three biggest is all growed up. We ain't seen hide ner hair of 'em since last fall. But we had a real treat last night," Maw hurried on. "Robbie Burns got married this winter, and we met our new daughter-in-law for the first time! She's a real fine girl."

Maw folded her hands in front of her. "No, there's just Rosie Pearl and Johnny Keats and the one on the way needing me now." She grinned self-consciously. "I do hope this one's a girl. I got one more real good girl's name left, Florabunda Emerald Bush."

Well, thank the good Lord for small blessings, I thought. *Maw's finally admitting out loud that she's expecting.* I glanced at Maggie. She winked at me.

38

I began thinking we might get to be friends after all when her mouth shaped a silent word: *Pregnant!* I turned away.

Robbie Burns's truck came rolling in about then. He came running across the parking area, waving his hat and shouting and towing Mavis behind him.

"The noisy one is Robbie Burns," Maw told Mrs. Campbell. "Mebbe you noticed, all our boys is named for poets and our girls for flowers and jewels?"

I looked quick-like at Maggie again. How could anyone miss the way she had named us? Especially Lily Opal and me. Flowers for first names and a last name like Bush?

Lily Opal and Buddy came walking, hand in hand, behind Robbie Burns and Mavis. I noticed again how kind of pulled into herself my sister looked.

When she'd married Buddy, two years ago, she'd stopped letting Paw cut her hair. Yesterday it had hung all the way down to her shoulders. Today she'd pinned it atop her head like an old woman. Yesterday she'd been wearing a gathered skirt with a shirt of Buddy's over it. Today she was wearing a pair of Buddy's overalls, with the shirt under them. The overalls were stretched tight over her middle, but they pretty much hung loose on her everywhere else.

"Good morning, Sis," I said. I wrapped my arms around her, then frowned. The bulge that was my niece or nephew, and Maw and Paw's first grandchild, was the only roundy spot on her. Lily Opal was thin as a rail.

"You okay?" I whispered. "You're awful skinny."

"Of course I'm okay. I'm just a mite tired."

She looked more than just tired to me. Hadn't Maw noticed?

But Maw just laughed. "This girl has no respect, Nellie. She's gonna make me a grandmaw before I'm through being a maw!"

39

Paw and Mr. Campbell were back now. The hugging and shouting started up again, just as if we hadn't all seen each other the night before.

Mrs. Campbell stammered weakly, "But—but—but—surely—"

"What's that, Nellie?" Maw shouted, leaning close. "Gotta speak up around this lot."

"But surely you and your daughter aren't picking strawberries in your delicate condition?" Mrs. Campbell blurted out.

Maw reared back with a shout. "None of us Bushes is what you'd call delicate. Of course Lily Opal's picking. But don't worry, Lily Opal and me will get some rest when we spell each other watching Johnny Keats."

But I found myself thinking the same as Mrs. Campbell. Delicate was just the right word for how Lily Opal looked.

Chapter 6

"Here comes the bus, Maw," Robbie Burns called.

Maw grabbed Mrs. Campbell's arm and beckoned to Maggie and me with the other. "You girls run get the shade hats," she said. "Nellie and me will get in line."

"What's the big hurry?" Maggie asked. She turned in a wide circle, looking at the fields all around us. "There's more strawberries than ten busloads of people could pick."

" 'Tain't that," I explained. "Old Porter purely hates it that we won't take his bus. Paw says he won't be bullied into paying to ride in that falling-apart rattletrap. With your father and mine sharing the gas money for our truck this season, we'll all ride cheaper than in Jake's bus, and safer, too."

As we got our hats out of the back of the truck, I added, "The reason we hurry to get near the front of the line is, if we're up near the foreman, Porter won't say nothing to us about the bus. You saw my paw yesterday," I reminded Maggie. "He ain't afraid of Jake Porter. But Paw don't go out of his way looking for trouble."

We started back to where our mothers were waiting. I found myself thinking about the look I'd seen on Jake's face the day before. I knew I was right about my paw not looking for trouble. I hoped that would be enough to mean there wasn't going to be any.

"Besides," I said, trying to forget Jake's face, "the Tates ride it, and I don't care to see Teddy again any sooner than I have to."

Maggie grinned. She probably thought I didn't like boys yet. That wasn't so. I just prefer boys who aren't so pushy. I'll bet my paw hadn't never been pushy with Maw when they were young and courting.

I glanced down at the hats I was carrying. I'd worn mine two summers now, and Lily Opal'd had it before that. The brim was all frayed, and the band around the crown was an old bandanna of Paw's. Maw's hat was even older. But the hats Maggie carried were brand-new.

I'd heard Mrs. Campbell tell Maw the day before that they'd sold almost everything they owned to get money and equipment for this trip. She'd also said they were only going to be migrants for this one summer. They planned to save money from picking to get them back East to Mr. Campbell's uncle's farm, where they could live and work until the depression ended.

I guess the Dust Bowl hadn't reached the farm they were going to. I wished our farm had been in the East.

I've heard lots of folks say that following the crops was just temporary for them. Most of them were still picking. Paw had said the same thing as we drove away from our farm that day. Out in the barn, the auctioneer had been selling off everything the bank wouldn't allow us to take.

When I looked up again, the bus was starting to unload.

"There's Teddy," Maggie said, poking me.

"And there's Betty Mae," I said happily.

"Who's Betty Mae?" Maggie asked.

"A friend from last year," I told her. "Look, Maggie, I promised Betty Mae I'd pick with her this summer. I'd best go tell her I'm already signed up to pick with you today."

I turned and ran down the lengthening line. "Betty Mae!" I shouted when I spotted her again. Teddy was still there, in front of her.

Betty Mae looked up when she heard her name. "Uh, hi, Rosie Pearl. I thought maybe you wasn't coming this season. When did you get here?"

"Late yesterday," I said, thinking, *She sure isn't acting very glad to see me.* "Look, Betty Mae," I said, "I know we promised to pick together this summer, but I hadn't seen you yet and I'm already signed up to pick today with a new girl."

"That's okay," Betty Mae said, a big smirk spread across her freckled face. "You go ahead and pick with your little friend. I'm gonna pick with Teddy!" She slipped her hand through Teddy's arm and smiled up at him.

The smirk on Betty Mae's face was sickening enough. The one on Teddy's was more than I could ignore.

Think, Rosie Pearl, I warned myself quickly. *Or this may be that time Maw meant—the day when you'll wish you hadn't ever learned to talk.*

I took a deep breath. "Hoo boy, ain't you a fast worker, Teddy." I tipped him a wink. "I just got rid of you last night, and you got a new girlfriend already!"

Betty Mae's smirk vanished. Her mouth dropped open.

As I made my way back to the head of the line, I could hear Betty Mae jawing away a mile a minute at Teddy. I smiled. Nope, I was right glad I still knew how to talk.

"Well, that's taken care of," I told Maggie. "Betty Mae has found herself someone else to pick with, so I guess you're stuck with me."

"You can switch if you want, Rosie Pearl," Maggie said. "I

know you're only picking with me because your mother said you have to.''

That embarrassed me a mite but I shook my head. "No, I'd really rather pick with you.''

"I'm glad,'' Maggie said. She was smiling that little crooked smile. Somehow it didn't look like a sneer anymore.

"Me too,'' I said, and I really meant it. Funny how things work out sometimes. I'd been waiting and waiting to see Betty Mae ever since we'd left Washington. How come I'd forgotten how boy-crazy she was? And what a sharp tongue she has?

"C'mon,'' I said, grabbing Maggie's hand. We ran to the front of the line, where the field foreman was giving out row assignments.

"Don't try to keep up with the Bushes your first day,'' he was saying to the Campbells. "They're the best and fastest pickers around!''

That made me feel real proud.

It still felt cool when I squatted down, facing Maggie across a row of strawberry plants. I reached out to pick my first berry of the season. Maggie reached, too, and her hat slipped down over her eyes.

"What a bother,'' she said impatiently. She snatched off the hat and dropped it on the ground beside her.

"Put it back on, Margaret,'' Mrs. Campbell called from several rows away, where she was picking with Mavis. Maw and Lily Opal were in the row beyond them, with Buddy and Mr. Campbell on their other side. Paw had gone off somewhere with Mr. Northrup to repair some machinery. I was glad. Paw got extra pay for those jobs.

"You'll get sunstroke,'' Mrs. Campbell warned as Maggie hesitated.

44

Maggie groaned and reached for her hat.

"She's right," I said quietly. "California sun's lots hotter than Washington sun. 'Tain't out of the ordinary here to see a picker passed out 'crost a row of berries."

I touched a sparkling drop of dew on a strawberry leaf. "By the end of the day, everything'll be dusty from us scrambling down the rows. Then they'll irrigate tonight, and we'll get muddy. 'Tain't easy keeping clean when you're picking." I sighed. "Matter of fact, ain't much of anything about this life that is easy."

I poked my fingers among the leaves and started picking, but Maggie lifted the leaves, then bent to peer under them. "You'll soon learn to feel which ones are ready to pick," I told her. "Drat! And which are like this one—already rotten!" I dropped the moldy berry in the dirt.

There was no answer from across the row. Maggie was picking like there was no tomorrow. Maybe she had taken what the foreman said as a dare, not a warning!

I had to slow her down. She was liable to kill herself off before lunch break. I picked up the rotten berry and threw it at Maggie. It hit her arm with a soft *splot.*

"What did you do that for, Rosie Pearl?" she shouted, scrubbing at the berry juice that dribbled down her arm.

"To get your attention," I said, leaning back and nibbling on a huge strawberry. "You know something, Maggie? I just purely love first day of picking. Course, by the end of the summer I don't never want to see another strawberry, raspberry, or green bean as long as I live." I could feel juice running down my chin as Maggie stared at me.

Her eyes widened and she ran her tongue over her dry lips. Then she turned and reached for the biggest berry in her box.

"Ah-ah," I warned. "Don't never eat from your box."

Startled, she asked, "Why not?"

"Paw says once a berry's in a box it belongs to whoever's buying that crop. But a berry on the plant belongs to whoever you're working for. This is one of Mr. Northrup's fields, and his pickers are always welcome to eat a few."

I started in on a second berry. "Another thing I like 'bout first day of picking is, nobody's pushing us yet. We can just kinda hunker back and take our own sweet time. So you can just slow down," I said with a grin. "This is first day of picking and I ain't racing with nobody!"

At lunch break, Teddy Tate came over to the tree we were eating under. I wasn't surprised. The way Betty Mae had jawed at him that morning, I was pretty sure she had dumped him just like I had.

But I was a mite surprised when he sat down next to Maggie. "Yer friend, Miss Bush, says I cain't talk to her," he said, peering around at me. "So what's yer name?"

She told him, and they talked back and forth. Then Maggie tried to get me to talk, too. "Did you know that, Rosie Pearl? Teddy's got more brothers than you do."

I bundled up my cold biscuits and molasses and flounced over to sit between Maw and Lily Opal.

Lily Opal kinda raised her eyebrows at me when I sat down, but she didn't say nothing. Maw was right in the middle of a story about something that had happened during the winter. I watched Lily Opal as she listened to Maw. Her eyes didn't have much life to them. Even her hair looked limp. My sister didn't seem to be taking too well to being pregnant. I'd started thinking that word, but still not saying it out loud, especially around Maw.

When Maw slowed down to take a bite, Lily Opal asked me

how I had done in school this past winter. I tried to give her good answers, but it was hard, seeing I was still trying to listen in on Maggie and Teddy.

It seemed like Teddy wanted me to be sure to hear, too, because he talked awful loud. When one of his brothers walked by, Teddy put his arm around Maggie and shouted, "Hey, Earl, c'mere and meet my new girlfriend, Maggie Murphy Magillacuddy McGee!"

Earl shook his head and walked on by. Maggie shoved Teddy's arm away and scrambled up, her face redder than Teddy's had ever been. She practically ran across to us. "Move over, Rosie Pearl," she said breathlessly.

"Sorry," I said sweetly. "There ain't room here for both you and your new boyfriend."

"Okay," she said through clenched teeth. "You were right! Now move over!"

I guess I waited a second too long because Lily Opal reached up and pulled Maggie down by her. "Don't you pay him no mind," she told Maggie. "He's just trying to copy his big brothers, and they was all terrible flirts."

"That's right," Maw agreed. "All but one of them come to their senses sooner or later. Teddy will, too, wait and see." Maw looked off into the distance.

"Well," I said, anxious to fill the silence. "I'm going to do my waiting from a good long distance."

"Me too," Maggie said.

That evening, after the supper dishes were done, Maggie and me were sitting out on the porch. "Wanta go play with the other kids?" I asked. "There's always two or three different games going on around camp."

Maggie stretched out her legs and groaned.

I laughed.

"What's so funny?" she asked crossly.

"You! Moaning and groaning like you was dying. I told you you'd be sore tonight. And on top of that, tomorrow you're gonna smell funny."

She sat up. "What?"

"Your Maw's gonna rub you down with good ol' smelly liniment tonight," I said.

"She is not!"

"She better had," I insisted. "Or you won't be able to walk at all. I'm gonna pick upwind of you tomorrow."

"My mother's not going to rub any nasty-smelling liniment on me, Miss Know-it-all. We don't have any."

Now I groaned and, moving slowly, got up. "Then I better go tell Maw. She's got a receipt for the best liniment around. Too bad it's the worst-smelling, too."

"Receipt?" Maggie asked.

"Maggie, don't you know nothing? A receipt is directions for making something."

"Rosie Pearl!" Maggie snapped back. "Don't *you* know nothing? That's a recipe. Nobody says *receipt* anymore. You do say the strangest things."

I whirled around and glared at her.

"Uhm, sorry, Rosie Pearl," Maggie said soothingly. "I'm sure your mother's receipt is wonderful."

I nodded shortly. "You better believe it!" I was nearly tempted not to tell Maw that the Campbells didn't have any liniment. That would teach Maggie to quit saying I was strange.

When we met on the porch next morning, Maggie raised her right hand and made it into a fist. "See that?" she asked. "Yeah."

"That's what I'm going to give you if you say one word about how I smell."

"Is that so?" I asked, stepping closer. "Take a whiff."

Maggie inhaled, then took a quick step backward.

I laughed. "Ain't we a pair?"

Chapter 7

That second morning of picking seemed to last forever. I waited at the end of a row for Maggie. She wasn't picking so fast today.

"Hey, don't pick slow on my account," she said, yawning.

"Didn't you sleep good last night?" I asked.

She shook her head. "Every time Mama or Papa turned over, I thought I was hearing a mouse I hadn't shaken out of the cornhusks. And my father's snoring sounds even worse in the cabin than it did in the tent."

I stood up and stretched my sore arms high above my head, then squatted down to start picking the next row of berries. I hadn't slept all that good myself. "You'll get used to it," I said in my best matter-of-fact voice. "You know any riddles?"

"Sure," she said. "What has four legs, but only one foot?"

"A bed," I shot back. "But not the ones in a pickers' camp. They only have two, because they're nailed to the wall."

She shrugged. "Guess that is kind of an old one. Your turn."

"Okay. What goes up, but never comes down?"

"Smoke," she said. "We're tied."

We swapped riddles for the next two rows. She'd heard some of mine, and I'd heard some of hers, but we each came up with some new ones. Next we talked about things we liked and things we hated. "I like chocolate ice cream," I started.

"Not me," Maggie said. "My favorite is strawberry." She looked at her stained hands and laughed. "At least it used to be."

"I hate washing dishes and getting up early," I said.

"Me too," Maggie said. Then she added softly, "And I hate leaving old friends and having to make new ones." She looked up at me. "At least, I used to."

I nodded in agreement. "Me too, but it's one of the things you get used to, following the crops." I thought for a minute. "Oh, yeah, something else I hate is getting a haircut. Maw cuts Paw's hair, but he cuts mine and Maw's and my brother's. If Maw don't watch him when he's cutting mine, I end up looking like a boy."

"I can't remember ever having more than just a trim," Maggie said thoughtfully. "One time I wanted bangs, and Mama cut them for me. But when I got tired of them, they took so long to grow out, I've never had her do it again."

"Paw says long hair's a luxury we can't afford," I said. "It takes too long to dry when you wash it, and it makes you sweat a lot on hot days in the field."

Maggie took off her hat and fanned herself. "You can say that again!"

"Paw says long hair's a luxury—" I started.

"Oh, shut up," she said. "I didn't mean you should really say all that again."

I laughed. "Yeah, I know."

We had picked along without saying anything for a few min-

51

utes when I noticed that Maggie had kind of a faraway look in her eyes. "What you thinking about?" I asked.

She shrugged and grinned. "Remember when we first met?"

"Yeah," I said. "It was only two days ago."

"I know. But it seems like we've known each other longer."

I nodded.

"Well," she went on, "remember what I said about the camp that day?"

Again I nodded. "You said it must be the worst place in the world."

She pressed her lips together, like she was trying to keep in her words, then said, "Well, it's not. Rosie Pearl, have you ever seen a Hooverville?"

"Can't say as I have," I said. "Where is it?"

"There are Hoovervilles all over the country, my papa says. But the one I saw was in Seattle. It's a town of little, rickety shacks built by folks who don't have anywhere else to live. They build the shacks out of pieces of wood and cardboard and tin— anything they can find. And mostly they build them by garbage dumps, because that's the best place to find building material."

I wrinkled up my nose, thinking what it would smell like to live next to a garbage dump. "Doesn't sound like anyplace I'd like to live," I said.

"It's not the kind of place anyone would like to live," Maggie said. "But some people have no choice. It's Hooverville or nothing. This place isn't much to brag about, but at least it's better than Hooverville." She looked up at me from under the brim of her hat. "I'm sorry I was such a snob that day, Rosie Pearl."

Now it was my turn to be embarrassed. "Aw, that's all right," I said, searching my mind for another riddle to change the subject again.

* * *

And that's the way life went, for several weeks. The same way it's gone for several years now. Get up early, eat, and dress. Ride to the fields shortly after sunup. Pick until noon. Eat lunch. Pick all afternoon. Ride back to the camp. Eat supper. Go to bed and sleep. And in the morning, get up and do it all over again, five and a half days a week.

There are good times, too. Like the after-supper games. Just before it gets true dark is the best time of day in a pickers' camp. For one thing, you can't see how shabby everything and everyone looks. For another, there's something special about playing games in the twilight of a California evening.

One other thing that breaks the monotony of the summer is going to town on a Saturday afternoon for supplies. I never have any money to spend, but it's fun to look around in the dime store and the drugstore. We have to be extra careful in those stores. The owners watch real close because some kids steal. And they aren't always kids from the camps.

But what really makes a summer bearable is having a friend across the row. Maggie became a good friend, over those weeks. We always seemed to find something new to talk about, when we both felt like talking. And when we didn't, the silence was just as comfortable as the silences I loved to share with my paw.

Then one afternoon, the field foreman asked me to finish off the last row in the corner of a field. "I don't know how it got overlooked," he said. "But there's some good berries there, maybe a full flat. I'll give you a double punch for each box, if you get all of them."

"Couldn't Maggie go, too?" I asked. "We're used to picking together."

He shook his head. "Sorry, Rosie Pearl. I know you, and I

53

know your family. But I've learned the hard way, two kids is often one kid too many.''

I was still pleased about getting a double punch for each box, so I went off cheerfully. Maggie picked with her maw that afternoon.

I was about half done with the forgotten berries when I heard someone coming up the row behind me. I turned, hoping the foreman had changed his mind and sent Maggie.

But it wasn't Maggie; it was the job boss, Jake Porter. Every morning Jake comes to the fields to make sure all the pickers show up. He seems to take special pleasure in yelling at anyone who's even a little late. And then he pops up here and there during the day, trying to show how important he is.

''Afternoon, little lady,'' Jake said.

''Afternoon,'' I answered, brief and polite. I looked down my row. Not far to go.

Jake stopped behind me and cleared his throat. I went on picking. ''Well now, Rosie Pearl,'' he said. ''Keepin' busy, are ya?''

''Yes sir.''

He walked around me and straddled the row I was picking. ''Busy people, alla yew Bushes,'' he said in a hard voice. ''''Cept that one, over there.''

I didn't look up, but I saw his shadow turn as he pointed off toward the trees where Lily Opal was resting.

He snickered. ''Reckon she'll be back to work, soon as she passes what's ailin' her.''

Passes what's ailing her? How could he talk about my sister's baby that way? I wanted to jump up and dump my whole flat of berries over his stupid head. I wanted to grind his greasy grin into the dirt. I wanted to shout every mean and nasty name I'd ever heard at him. But I didn't do any of those things. I kept shut because I felt glued to the ground with mortification.

But Jake wasn't through. "Cain't complain, though," he went on. "Every migrant born's a new picker fer me in a few years."

A picker for *him*? To hear Jake Porter tell it you'd think he owned these fields instead of just getting crews together for them that did. Pickers respect the job, they just don't respect Jake Porter. And I was getting an earful of why.

"Shucks, before yew know it yew'll be gettin' married and havin' babies, and I'll have to be findin' them jobs, too."

In spite of myself, I glanced up. Jake looked same as always: stubbly chin, greasy hair, wooden match sticking out of the corner of his mouth, dirty checked vest stretched tight over his potbelly.

"Mebbe yew should start lookin' around fer a man with a good job who could be givin' yew those babies, Rosie Pearl."

All of a sudden it felt like the middle of a Yakima winter. I was so cold I thought I'd never thaw out, just squatting there in the dirt.

Now I'm not stupid. I catch on right quick when a grown-up says something in a roundabout sort of way. Jake Porter was saying he could give me babies!

I don't know how I got my hands moving again, but I ducked my head and went back to picking like Jake wasn't there. *That's what Paw would have told me to do,* I thought. *Of course, if Paw was here, Jake wouldn't be talking to me at all!*

"Yessiree," Jake continued. "Yew migrants is mighty fine breeders. Yew he'p keep me supplied with pickers." He paused. I guess he expected me to say something now. When I didn't, his voice turned angry.

"And don't go thinkin' yer any better'n the rest, just 'cause I stopped to talk to yew, Miss High-and-Mighty! Yew and yer brats and their brats'll be pickin' in these fields long as there's crops to pick. Ain't one of yew got backbone enough to be nuthin' but migrants!"

55

The cold passed; I knew my face must be blazing red. Behind me stretched cleanly picked rows. Ahead of me was a broom's length of unpicked berries and Jake Porter.

Hands shaking, I reached for the next berry. Jake moved forward. Now I couldn't pick without touching him. *I'd rather touch a dead skunk,* I thought, closing my eyes.

Teddy chased me with a dead skunk once. He'd found it on the highway. That poor critter was flat as a pancake and dried hard as the cow pies Robbie Burns and Walter Scott used to sail out in our pasture. But it still stunk to high heaven.

My stomach lurched. I knew if Jake touched me I'd throw up on his feet, just like I did that time to Teddy. I almost laughed out loud, recollecting the look on Teddy's face as the wet warmth had spread across his bare feet and seeped down between his toes.

I looked at the frayed cuffs of Jake's trousers. "I'd rather touch a dead skunk," I said solemnly.

Jake drew in a sharp breath, and I clapped my hand over my mouth. My shoulders tensed. I just knew he was going to yell at me. Maybe even hit me! As I waited I suddenly realized that Maw had been right again. The day had come when I wished I had never learned to talk!

But Jake didn't say or do anything.

"Is there some reason you're keeping my daughter from her work, Porter?" came Paw's quiet voice.

Not waiting for an answer, Paw said, "Finish off your row, Rosie Pearl. I'll help you tote your flat to the shed. I need to have a word with the field foreman."

The silence above me as I picked was so deep I thought I could hear the berries letting go as I pulled them hurriedly from the plants. Out of the corner of my eye I could see Jake's shadow backing off down the row.

"What was he saying to you?" Paw asked when we were halfway across the field. Before I could say a word, I began trembling. There was an awful buzzing in my head. Startled, I saw the ground coming up at me. Everything went black.

When I opened my eyes, I was in my bunk. Maw was putting a cold, wet cloth on my forehead.

"What happened?" I asked weakly.

"Shhh," Maw said soothingly. "You fainted. It ain't nothing unusual for a hot day like this."

And then I remembered. It wasn't the hot day that had made me faint. It was the absolute terror I'd felt, squatting there in the dirt at Jake Porter's feet. But Paw must have let Maw think it was the heat.

"Just rest easy now," Maw said. "I'm gonna start supper."

I sighed, watching Maw shake up the coals in the black iron cookstove. I knew that after supper Paw would suggest something for Maw and Johnny Keats to do so he could talk to me about Jake Porter.

I'd given up trying to lie to Paw when I was about Johnny Keats's age, and I wasn't going to lie to him now. But I knew I couldn't tell him everything Jake had said or the sly way he'd said it.

Like saying Lily Opal would feel better when she passed what ailed her. And calling migrants breeders, like we was animals. But especially how we'd all go on being migrants because none of us had the gumption to be anything better.

Even Jake's ridiculous hint about giving me babies hadn't got me as mad as his saying I didn't have any gumption. I've got plenty. And so does the rest of my family.

Sure enough, after supper, while Maw was hanging up the wet

dishtowels, Paw said, "Did you take that reel of sewing thread over to Lily Opal yet, Edith?"

"Not yet," she replied. "She ain't in no hurry for it. I'll set a spell first."

"No," Paw said firmly. "Now. And take Johnny Keats with you."

She turned and looked at Paw, her blue eyes dark and snapping. "Look here, Orrin," she started. Then she stopped, and nothing seemed to happen for several seconds.

I didn't even know I'd been holding my breath until Maw let hers go with a loud *whoosh.* "Good idea," she said quietly. "Then when I come back I won't have to get up again until bedtime."

Johnny Keats looked back over his shoulder as Maw hurried him out the door. *I'd rather you stayed, too,* I thought, waving at him.

Paw came and sat on my bunk. "Feel good enough to talk now, Rosebud?"

"I guess so, Paw."

"Then tell me what Jake Porter said to you."

"He said all of us Bushes was hard workers," I said in a small voice. "All but Lily Opal—right now."

"He remarked on your sister's condition?"

I looked down at my hands. "Yeah."

Paw's voice was hard and tight. "What else?"

"Well . . ." I hesitated, wishing I could pull my quilt up over my head. But Paw wasn't going to be put off that easy.

"He was standing there a long time, Rosebud," Paw said. "He must have said more than just that."

"Uhm, he said he supposed Lily Opal would be back to working full-time after she had her baby and that the baby would be a good picker, too, once it got big enough."

58

"And that's all he said?" Paw was talking quietly, but his jaw was so tight, there were white spots on his cheeks.

"That's about it, Paw," I insisted, plucking at the tufts of yarn Maw had tied in each quilt square. "Maybe not word for word, but that's what he talked about—migrants and picking and that sort of stuff."

Paw shook his head. "There's something more, Rosie Pearl. Something you ain't told me yet."

I clutched the coverlet tighter. *Don't ask me any more,* I begged silently. *Please, Paw, don't ask!*

"I couldn't see Porter's face, coming up behind him like I did," Paw went on. "But he was mad about something, clenching his hands. And from the look on your face, when you put your hand 'crost your mouth, you was scared!"

Then I had an idea. Paw knew about the skunk, and me throwing up on Teddy's feet. Maybe I could distract him if I told about being afraid Jake was going to touch me, and saying out loud, "I'd rather touch a dead skunk."

As I'd hoped, Paw laughed about the skunk and didn't ask any more questions.

When Maw and Johnny Keats came back, Paw and me were still laughing and giggling in fits and starts.

"Well," Maw said, "if you two was going to have a laughing party you might have invited the rest of us. There ain't that much to laugh about around here."

At bedtime, when Paw came over to my bunk to kiss me good-night, he said, "I'm right proud of the way you acted today, Rosebud."

"Thanks, Paw," I said, relieved that the questions were over. But I also felt a mite nervous over not having told him everything.

Chapter 8

I didn't pick the next day; Maw made me stay in bed. I'd have enjoyed the day off if I hadn't been all alone. Everyone else still had to work. Maggie brought me her copy of *Little Women*. I was so glad to have it. I'd long ago outgrown the two books I'd brought with me when we left the farm. I'd read *Felix the Cat* five times, then handed it on to Johnny Keats. I'd even read that newspaper I found with the funnies. That left Maw's Sunday School Bible as the only reading material in our cabin. I'd read all the best parts of that when I had the measles.

Maggie's book helped the time go a little faster. The family in that book had some hard times, too, but they had some times for laughing, just like me and my family.

Buddy drove Lily Opal home at lunchtime, then went back to the fields. She got kind of cross with him for taking the time, and gas, to bring her all the way back to camp. But all Buddy said was, "I've had a talk with your paw, honey. It's best this way."

I was glad Lily Opal was out of Jake Porter's sight. And I was glad to have some company. Maw had left some soup on the back of the stove for our lunch. Lily Opal dished it up and set it on the table.

"You need to eat more than that," I said, looking down at my full bowl and hers with just the bottom covered.

Her head snapped up. "Don't *you* start on me," she said. "You're as bad as Maw and Buddy!"

My spoon dropped on the table. My sister never talked to me like that.

"Aw, baby, I'm sorry. I just don't have much appetite lately."

"That's awright," I said. "I guess it ain't easy being pregnant." I picked up my spoon and took a sip.

"Pregnant!" Lily Opal shouted. This time my spoon landed on the floor. "Pregnant?" She leaned back on her stool and began to laugh.

I looked at her for a couple of seconds, then I giggled. Pretty soon tears were running down our faces, we were both laughing so hard.

Lily Opal wiped her eyes on a rag from her pocket. "Rosie Pearl, you better not say that word in front of Maw."

"I know," I said, wiping mine on the tail of Paw's old shirt that I used as a nightgown. "She'd wear me out for sure."

"You're really growing up, Little Sis," Lily Opal said quietly.

"I reckon so."

Lily Opal chuckled again; then she clutched her stomach and got a real surprised look on her face. "Oooh, that was a hard one," she said.

"A hard what?" I demanded. "What's wrong?"

She smiled. "Nothing's wrong, Little Sis. The baby just gave me a good hard kick. Reckon he or she thinks it's time for a rest." She beckoned me closer. "Want to feel?"

Cautiously I rested my hands where hers had been. At first all I felt was a tiny shimmering, like wind blowing across water. Then, short and quick as the tap of a hammer, something hit the palm of my hand. I jumped. "Wow!" I shouted. "What was that?"

Lily Opal shrugged. "A hand or a foot. Maybe an elbow. You ought to feel it from this side."

"No thanks," I said. "This'll do me for now."

"Well," Lily Opal said, getting slowly to her feet, "maybe you better not tell Maw I let you feel my stomach. She doesn't think you need to know about such things yet."

Such things? If Maw thought I was too young to be feeling Lily Opal's baby kick, I wonder what she'd think about what Jake had said to me. Oh well, she wasn't going to hear about either one. Not the way she worried about such things.

Before Lily Opal left, she nodded toward Maggie's book. "Maw says you're to take a nap now," she said. "And so are we." She went next door and I was alone again.

For days after I went back to work, I kept glancing around, half expecting to see Jake standing there again. But I didn't have to see him to remember his words: "Ain't one of yew got backbone enough to be nuthin' but migrants."

It wasn't as if I liked being a migrant. It's hard, dirty work. I only make about fifty cents a day. It can be dangerous, too, because there are all kinds of strange folks following the crops.

Some of the men get discouraged and start spending what little they do earn on whiskey. Women start going from cabin to cabin, asking for something to feed their children. Then the husbands go to beating their wives for shaming them so.

Some people who work the crops lie and steal, and others bully, like Jake Porter. And every once in a while there's an unexplained death. Like the one I read about in Paw's newspaper. It had happened at a camp farther south. We picked there once. Paw hadn't read that part out loud. Funny, I never saw that newspaper again after Paw saw me reading it. Maw and Paw try to keep such things from me and Johnny Keats, but gossip spreads through the camps quicker than a grass fire.

I knew there were lots of jobs Paw would rather be doing. Ones where his wife and children wouldn't have to work so hard. But I hadn't known I was supposed to be ashamed of what we were doing. At least, Jake Porter seemed to think I should.

Maw and Paw always tell us to do our best, no matter what the job. Wasn't that why the foreman had asked me to finish off that field? He knew I would do a good job.

But Jake Porter said I was going to be a migrant for the rest of my life. And my children, too. All of a sudden, I didn't want to be a migrant anymore, and there wasn't a thing I could do about it.

One thing had changed. Whatever Paw said to the field foreman that day, it made a difference. Jake Porter didn't come into the fields to talk to the pickers anymore. He did walk around the edge of every field with his clipboard each morning, making a big show out of checking off names. I wasn't the only one who turned my back to him.

Seeing him, even far off like that, kept his words rising to the top of my mind, like cream on a bottle of milk. But his words didn't taste like cream; they tasted like a big swallow of milk that has gone bad.

I'd always liked myself just fine before this. Sure, I've got some faults. Doesn't everybody, if they're honest? But now, for the first time ever, I felt uneasy with who I was. And even more uneasy with who I was going to be, someday.

I must have been thinking those thoughts more than I realized, because a couple of evenings later at the supper table, Maw said, "You feeling awright, Rosie Pearl? You've been mighty quiet lately."

"I'm fine, Maw," I said. "I'm just trying to take your advice about thinking before I talk." That seemed to satisfy Maw, but I caught Paw looking at me kind of strange a couple of times.

When we were through eating, Paw stood up and reached for his pipe. After he filled the bowl with tobacco, he waited for me to strike a wooden match on the top of the stove and hold it out.

"How about a little walk after you do up the dishes, Rosebud?" he asked between puffs.

"Okay, Paw." I was pretty sure he was going to ask more questions. And I was surprised to find that I was glad.

Several times in the past days, I'd wished I had told Paw all of it the first time. Then maybe these bad feelings I was having because of Jake's words would have been gone.

I got the dishpan from its nail on the wall and filled it with soap and hot water. It would soon be over with now.

"Porter said things you ain't told me yet, Rosebud," Paw said as we started out. "Ready to talk about them now?"

I grabbed his hand and matched my steps to his. "Yes, Paw," I started. "But how come, if you know I didn't tell you everything, you ain't mad at me?"

Paw squeezed my hand. "You weren't keeping it back to be bad, Rosebud."

I nodded. "That's right, Paw. I could tell you was real upset when I told you that Porter was talking to me about Lily Opal having a baby. . . ."

Paw's hand tightened again, then relaxed. "This is 1936, Rosebud. The world is changing fast, mebbe too fast. But your maw and me was raised to treat such things as family business."

Hoo boy, didn't I know that!

"And Jake Porter, of all people," Paw went on. "Why, he's
. . . he's so . . . he's so, so confounded, dingbusted . . .
Rude!"

"Rude!" I shrieked, hardly able to believe my ears. *"Rude's*
the only word you can think of to call Jake Porter?"

Paw's face turned red. "No, Rosebud, there's lot of names I'd
like to call Jake. But I wouldn't use none of 'em in front of my
daughter."

I laughed. "Shucks, I thought I'd learn me something new."

Paw laughed. I should have known better than to worry and
keep all this to myself. Still, one last bit of caution made me ask,
"You sure you want to hear it all, Paw?"

He turned me to face him. "Honey, it ain't that I need to hear
it so much as you need to get rid of the weight of it. It about kills
me to see you so burdened."

I took a deep breath. "Okay, but you're gonna get mad."

Paw took my hand again. He swung it back and forth as we
walked along the edge of a field. "Mebbe I will, but not at you."

So I began again. "The first thing Jake talked about was how
Lily Opal would be able to work again after she had her baby.
But did he have to say 'passing what ails her,' like the baby was
just a bad case of indigestion? Then he said how we was all good
breeders. Paw, that kind of talk makes migrants sound like nothing but animals!"

I was looking down at my feet as we walked. I hadn't known
I'd still be shy about looking at Paw when I told him these
things, but I was. He didn't speak, so I went on.

"The next thing he said was really disgusting. He said I
should start looking around for a husband with a good job so I
could be having babies. You know what, Paw? He was hinting
that he could be my husband and give me babies. Ain't that
disgusting?"

I glanced up. Paw's forehead and cheeks were bright red, but

65

his teeth were clenched so tight, his jaw was dead white. "Is that all of it?" he asked.

"Almost," I said, my voice shaking a little. "What I've already told you bothered me, Paw. But, after a while, I begun to forget it. 'Cause, ain't that just the kind of thing Jake Porter says, nasty, mean, and disgusting, like him, but not worth paying any mind to?

"What's really been worrying at me was that he said none of us had enough backbone to ever be nothing but migrants. Oh, Paw," I said, my voice getting all quivery, "what if it's true?"

I looked up. Paw's whole face had turned white. The grip of his hand hurt so much I flinched and almost hollered. He let loose of my hand, but the look on his face kept me silent.

Looking down, he nudged at a stone with the toe of his heavy boot. "Oh, God," he muttered. "Dear God in heaven, sometimes it's more than a man can bear!"

He picked up the stone and heaved it at a fencepost. A big chunk of the post flew off and landed in the field. Paw kept on picking up stones and heaving them. Soon there were no more stones, but still he searched frantically through the ruts and weedy roadside.

I got scared! I tugged at his shirt. "Paw," I choked out. "Oh, Paw, stop! Please stop, you're scaring me."

First thing I knew he had his arms around me and I was bawling like a baby. But Paw didn't cry. He just held me. Sometimes I wonder what it would be like to be as strong as my paw and never cry.

When I'd sorta run down, Paw set me down in the grass and handed me a faded rag. He started to talk quietly, the color coming back into his face. "You're right about paying no mind to most of what Jake says. I'm proud of you for being growed up enough to know that. But there's something else you need to know about Jake Porter. This is the best job he's ever had. He's so scared of losing it, he spends most of his time trying to make people feel like they're less than him."

Paw was right. I'd known that was what Jake was doing, I just hadn't known why.

"But mark my words," Paw went on. "One day Jake Porter will look up and there won't be a single member of the Bush family in sight. It won't happen all at once, Rosebud, just a little at a time. Like the Perkinses' oldest boy not coming back to pick this summer because he found a permanent job. Someday it'll be your turn. Someday you won't have to put up with rude men like Jake Porter."

I smiled, trying to guess what other names Paw would rather be calling Jake.

"Say now!" Paw said in a teasing tone. "You found something to be happy about? Tell me. I could use some cheering up."

I told Paw what I'd been trying to guess. A little smile turned up the corners of his mouth.

As we headed back to camp, I asked, "Paw, you're not gonna do anything to Jake, are you?"

He shook his head. "No, there ain't nothing to be gained from that. He's probably already figured out that I told the field foreman I didn't like him bothering you. Anyway, it's the foreman's job to take complaints to the growers. That's the proper way."

I sighed with relief. "Thanks for the talk, Paw."

We walked home, swinging our hands again, and I wondered if Paw was right. Would it really be my turn someday?

Chapter 9

The next morning, as we started on the first of the raspberries, I chattered away to Maggie. "I been thinking. If I ever do up and get married, I'm gonna marry a man who works in the city. One who gets up in the morning and puts on a suit with a vest and then goes off downtown to work in an office. That's another reason I don't want to marry Teddy Tate. He wants to be a farmer, if this depression ever gets over and he can buy some land."

It was quiet on the other side of the row. I looked up.

"Welcome back!" Maggie cried.

"What are you talking about?" I questioned. "Maggie, I ain't gone anyplace. I've been right here across the row from you, every day, for weeks now."

She shook her head. "Someone's been there all right, but it didn't seem to be you. Might as well have been some town kid for all the company you were."

"I had something on my mind," I admitted. "But my paw helped me work it out. Most of it anyway."

"That's good," she said. "I knew something was missing, but I didn't know it was your mind." She picked faster. "Picking can be lonesome work when you're alone."

I sighed. "Tell me about it. You only have to pick this one summer. After you get to your great-uncle's, you'll never have to be a migrant again."

"Rosie Pearl!" Maggie said angrily. "I'm just beginning to feel like I fit in here. Don't say that I'm different."

"But you are different," I insisted. "You don't dress like a migrant. You don't talk like a migrant. You don't think like a migrant. You know why?"

She glared at me. "No, why?"

"Because you *ain't* a migrant!" I shouted. "So don't go around trying to be what you ain't!" I buried my face in my stained hands. My voice was muffled, but she heard me. "Don't you know how lucky you are?"

"Well . . . sure . . . of course I do." She was talking softer, too. "But, Rosie Pearl, you make it sound so awful."

Maybe it was because she sounded like she cared, like she really wanted to know. Maybe it was because I'd never before thought about doing this for the rest of my life.

I heard myself saying, in a tight voice, "I don't wanna be a migrant for the rest of my life."

"Then don't be," Maggie said. "Be something else."

"But Jake Porter said . . ." And the whole story tumbled out.

Maggie listened in shocked silence. "That dirty old man!" she said.

"Paw says Jake likes to make other people feel like nothing. That's how he builds himself up, and that's why he said I'd never be nothing but a migrant."

I hesitated. "I want Paw to be right," I said at last. "But I'm afraid that Jake Porter's the one who's right."

"Well, he's not," Maggie said emphatically. "Not about you. I don't care what you call it—backbone, gumption, or spunk—you've got more of it than any other girl I know."

Tears filled my eyes. "You really think so?"

She nodded and began to pick even faster.

I slowed down a little, to let her catch up. "Paw always says I've got the most gumption of any of us." I brightened up a bit at my next thought. "Maggie, you got any ideas on how I could set about becoming something else?"

"Not right this minute," she said. "But I'll bet, if we put our heads together, we could come up with lots of ideas."

That night at supper Maw remarked about the change in me. "Got your appetite back, Rosie Pearl?"

I reached for another piece of corn bread. "Sure have, Maw."

After I washed the dishes, I went outside. Maggie was sitting on the edge of the porch, swinging her legs.

I sat down next to her. "What you doing?"

"Just thinking about what you said about me not dressing or talking or thinking like a migrant."

"Well, you don't!"

"I know that. But maybe if you stopped dressing or talking or thinking like a migrant, pretty soon you wouldn't be one, either."

I looked down at my knickers. "Can't do much about the way I dress," I said.

"No," Maggie agreed. "But you could start with the way you talk."

"What's wrong with the way I talk?"

She threw up her hands. "Hey, don't get mad at me! You're the one who said I don't talk like a migrant. Doesn't that mean you do? So, stop talking like a migrant."

A minute or two went by while I thought about that. "You might be right," I said. "But I'd sure need a heap of help!"

Maggie looked up and down the long porch. I looked, too. There wasn't anyone close. "Have I ever told you that my mother taught school before she married my father?" she asked. "What she doesn't know about grammar isn't worth knowing."

"Oh, no," I said, jumping down from the porch. "I like your maw—she's a real nice lady. But I get all skitterish and tongue-tied around teachers—even ones that ain't teaching anymore."

"I didn't mean my *mother* should help you," Maggie said. "I can do that. But if I get stuck for the right way to say something, all I have to do is say it the way you do around my mother and she'll correct me."

"You mean purposely say something the wrong way in fronta your maw? You'd do that for me?"

"Sure," she said. "It'd be fun. Mama would think I was picking up bad habits."

" 'Tain't good to worry your maw needless-like."

"I know," she said with a little grin. "But I'll say it the right way after that, to show her I've learned my lesson. She'll be so pleased, she'll forget she was ever worried."

I laughed so hard Maw stuck her head out of our cabin to shush me. When she was gone, I said, "Ain't you a caution!"

"Ain't I, though!" Maggie said. Then she looked thoughtful.

"What now?" I asked.

"Well, I'm thinking it's all right for Mama to correct me when there's other people around; she's my mother. But I can't do that to you."

"No," I agreed. "I wouldn't like that."

"How about if we have a secret signal when other people are around," Maggie suggested. "We could make a game out of it."

"What kinda game?" I asked. Lots of times teachers say something is going to be a game, but it hardly ever turns out to be much fun. "What kinda game?" I asked again.

"Well," Maggie said slowly. "How about when I hear you say something wrong, I give you a secret signal. Then, if you can figure out what you said wrong and say it right, that's one point for you. But if you don't, it's one point for me."

"What does the winner get?" I asked.

"I don't know yet," Maggie said. "Neither of us has any money. But I'll think of something."

"Okay. And I've got an idea for the secret signal. Want to hear it?"

"Sure."

I giggled to myself. "You're gonna love this! Paw usta do it when these awful neighbors came to visit back on the farm. They'd stay as long as Maw kept pouring coffee and bringing out cookies or cake. When Paw had got his fill of their company, he'd look at Maw and rub the side of his nose, like this." I showed Maggie what I meant.

"But how would that get rid of them?" Maggie asked.

"Well, when Maw saw Paw rubbing his nose, she would look around the kitchen and say something like, 'Goodness, I ain't gonna be able to feed my family if I don't get this kitchen cleaned up.'

"And Paw would say, 'And just look at that woodbox. Edith ain't gonna have no wood to cook with if I don't bring in a couple of armloads.' "

Maggie frowned. "I still don't see how that would get rid of anybody."

I laughed. "That's because you don't know how bone-lazy these folks were. When they heard Maw or Paw talk about any kinda work, Henry would turn to his wife and say, 'Well,

Lucindy, we're jest in the way 'round here. It's time we was gettin' home, so these folks can get their chores done.' And quick as a wink, they was gone!''

We laughed over that so hard, Maw stuck her head out the door again. ''Say good-night, Rosie Pearl, it's bedtime.''

''Okay, Maw,'' I said. ''Good night, Maggie. Sleep tight, don't let the bedbugs bite.''

''You shut up about bedbugs,'' Maggie snapped, clapping her hand over my mouth.

''Okay,'' I mumbled through her fingers.

''Then, good night, and sleep tight yourself,'' she said, taking her hand away. ''And tomorrow you're going to start learning not to say *ain't*.''

''Yes, teacher,'' I said in my sassiest voice.

She grinned and strutted down the porch. ''Maybe I *should* be a teacher, like my mother's always hinting.'' She whisked through her cabin door.

I went in to bed, too, wondering if I'd done a dumb thing, agreeing to let Maggie help me with the way I talk.

As I climbed into the back of the truck next morning, Maggie winked at me and patted the pocket of her overalls. ''Wait until you see what I've got for a prize,'' she said softly.

''Show me!''

She shook her head. ''Not until we're alone.''

''Oooooh, Maggie,'' I squealed, pretending to be shocked. ''You ain't gone and stole something, have you?''

She rolled her eyes. ''Don't be silly,'' she said. She sat down carefully, hand cupped around her pocket. ''Don't want to break it.''

I plopped down next to her, my curiosity flaring like a case of poison ivy.

Johnny Keats and Maggie's folks got in back with us. Lily Opal and Maw rode in front with Paw.

"And besides . . ." Maggie rubbed a finger along the side of her nose.

"Hey," I objected. "I'm barely outta bed. My oatmeal ain't even had time to reach my stomach. You can't expect me to watch what I'm saying this early."

"Oh yes I can. And besides . . ." She straightened a second finger and rubbed her nose with both of them.

Oh, no! Two mistakes already? It didn't matter how good a prize Maggie had in her pocket. I was never going to win it at this rate.

I thought a minute, then said quickly, "What I meant to say was, my oatmeal hasn't hardly had time to reach my stomach yet."

She leaned back, hands behind her head. "That's one point for each of us."

"Hold on a minute," I complained. "Don't rush me." But no matter how hard I thought, I couldn't remember what other time I had said *ain't.*

"I give up," I said when we got to the fields. "Now show me what's in your pocket."

"Not until we're *alone,*" she said again.

As soon as we were assigned our rows, I hurried Maggie across the field and dropped my wooden flat at the end of the first row. One of the little boxes the berries go to the store in popped out. I shoved it quickly back in place and held out my hand. "We're as alone as we're gonna get," I growled. "Let's see it!"

Maggie pulled her hand out of her pocket. She held out her closed fist. Slowly, finger by finger, she opened it and dropped a round object into my hand. As I looked down at it, the sun peered through the trees at the end of the field. I gasped. I was holding a round rainbow!

I looked up to see her pleased smile. "Maggie, is this yours?" I asked.

"Sure is," she said proudly. "It's the brooch my grandma wore when she married my grandpa. She got it from her grandma, so she left it to me."

"But—but—Maggie," I stammered. "You can't give away your inheritance."

"I wasn't expecting to. Would it seem like enough of a prize to you if the one who has the most points each night could wear it the next day?"

"Sure!" I looked down again. The sun had moved and taken my rainbow with it. But the circle of stones with all their tiny flat surfaces now glowed bloodred. "Are they rubies?" I asked.

"No, they're garnets. But they're set in fourteen-karat gold, and—"

"Rosie Pearl?" came a deep voice behind us. I jumped, closing my hand so fast the pin on the brooch dug into my palm. It was Mr. Northrup, owner of the raspberry bushes we were supposed to be picking.

"What are you two up to?" he asked.

Chapter 10

Mr. Northrup is my favorite of all the owners in the Valley Growers' Association. I think my family is one of his favorites, too. We pick at his fields most of the summer. The only time we work for someone else is if he doesn't have a crop ready to pick.

Even though I like him, I'm a little nervous around him. He's a kinda quiet man, like my paw. I've known my paw all my life, so his quietness doesn't bother me. But I'm never quite sure what Mr. Northrup is thinking. He's way up there over everyone, even Jake Porter, who just thinks he's better than the pickers.

So when he says something like ''What are you two up to?'' I don't know if I'm in trouble or not.

''I ain't up to nothing,'' I said, opening my hand. ''I'm just looking at Maggie's brooch.''

Mr. Northrup looked at Maggie. His tanned forehead was wrinkled into a frown. His mouth was working hard not to smile. I couldn't believe he was really angry.

''You're Ed and Nellie Campbell's daughter, right?'' he asked Maggie.

"Yes sir," she said. Then, when he glanced down at the brooch in my hand, she began rubbing her nose.

That Maggie! She has no idea about the proper time to be playing games.

"That's a pretty thing," Mr. Northrup said. "Too nice to be carrying around in the fields. It could get lost very easily."

"You're right," Maggie agreed. "That's why I was just about to put it away." She took the brooch and slipped it into her pocket. Then she pinned the pocket shut with a big safety pin.

"That's better," Mr. Northrup said.

I grabbed a berry box from my flat and started to pick. "We'd better get on with getting these raspberries picked, Maggie. That's what we're here for."

Mr. Northrup chuckled. "I like your attitude, Rosie Pearl. But it doesn't surprise me. There's no complainers or shirkers in your family. Once this depression's over, well, who knows what you all might go on to do?"

Surprised, I turned to watch him walk away. "How about that!" I exclaimed. "That was a real nice thing for him to say."

"He thinks well of your family," Maggie said. "If I were you, I'd believe what he says, not that sleazy old Jake Porter."

I wanted to agree. But, as Maw's so fond of saying, words once spoke can't be taken back. It would be a long time before I forgot what Jake had said.

My hands were moving faster now. That brooch was one of the prettiest things I had ever seen. It must be worth a lot of money. What was that word Maw had used when I forgot to lock the food box? *Responsible,* that was it. Did I want to be responsible for the brooch Maggie's grandma had given her?

"Maggie?" I asked.

"Yeah?"

"Mr. Northrup is right about that brooch. It's too fine to wear in a berry field."

77

Maggie glared at me across the row. "Rosie Pearl Bush, this is *my* brooch. I'll decide when it's to be worn and by who. I mean, by *whom*."

I burst out laughing. "Okay, I'll carry the brooch when I win, pinned up tight in my pocket. But you've got to promise to just teach me one thing at a time. It's hard enough learning not to say *ain't*. I'm not ready for *who* and *whom*."

$\mathcal{I}$t took me almost two weeks to get used to not saying *ain't*, and another two to straighten out *was* and *were*. Nobody remarked about me talking different, but I noticed Paw paying extra attention when I talked. One night at the supper table he grinned at me and winked. Still, being Paw, he didn't say nothing, I mean anything.

Maggie and me were just about even at first. She'd carry the brooch one day and I would have it the next. Then the berries ran out, and we moved to picking apricots and peaches. Now I carried it twice, then three times as often as she did.

I felt right proud of myself, maybe too proud. One day, just before noon, I'd filled my bushel basket with apricots. Maggie's still had a ways to go, so I sat down to wait for her. "You go on," she said. "Find us a shady spot to eat lunch."

"Okay." I picked up my basket and walked to the shed, where the field foreman punched my tally card. Shirley Jean, one of the high-school pickers from town, was leaning against a wall talking to the foreman's good-looking helper.

Several other pickers followed me into the shed, so the foreman's helper turned his back on Shirley Jean and began punching cards.

Shirley Jean glared at me like it was my fault he wasn't talking to her anymore.

The kids who stay in the camps don't hang around with the

kids from town. And the townies don't have much to do with us, either.

So I was surprised when Shirley Jean said teasingly, "What's that pinned in your pocket, little girl? A hankie?"

In the past I'd have ignored her. I wouldn't have cared that nobody in my family even owned a hankie.

But I'd been thinking too much about Jake Porter's words. I hadn't forgotten what Mr. Northrup said either. I just wasn't sure which one was right.

I stared at Shirley Jean, wanting to be the kind of person with a clean hankie in her pocket every day of the week.

I felt my mouth smile, knowing the smile didn't reach my eyes. Shirley Jean pushed away from the wall and walked over to me. "Oh, now I see. It's too big to be a hankie. It must be your lunch."

Still looking straight at her, I fumbled to unpin my pocket. I pulled out the brooch and held it where a ray of sunshine could shine on it. Shirley Jean's mouth dropped open.

"Slowpoke," Maggie scolded as she entered the shed. She slid her basket onto the counter and handed her card to the foreman. "We'll have to hurry if we want a place in the shade now," she said, grabbing the punched card and hurrying out into the hot sunshine.

I dropped the brooch back into my pocket and followed.

We had a special good time at lunch that day. We even picked up some new riddles by eavesdropping on the townies.

Only one thing happened to spoil it. That was Jake Porter walking by. "You'd think he could leave us alone when we're eating," I said. "That man purely makes me sick at my stomach."

At the end of the day we climbed slowly into the back of Paw's truck. "You get to keep the prize another day, Rosie

Pearl,'' Maggie said. She propped herself up in a corner. ''You have the most points again.''

We had agreed that the game wouldn't start until we got to the fields. That way I wouldn't have to be correcting myself around our families. We stopped when we started home from the fields. We were both too tired by then to do much thinking.

''Don't feel bad,'' I said, around a huge yawn. ''You're a real good teacher.'' I reached to pat my pocket before I sat down. It felt awfully flat.

Maggie pulled at the leg of my knickers. ''Sit down before you fall down.''

Sometimes I called her Maw when she bossed me like that. But I had trouble opening my mouth this time. I was afraid my heart would fall out of it.

''In a minute,'' I croaked. ''I forgot something in the shed.'' I jumped off the end of the truck. As I ran toward the shed, I reached into my pocket. No wonder it felt so flat—it was empty! Someplace between the shed and the truck I had lost Maggie's inheritance!

''What did you forget?'' Maggie called.

''My hat,'' I called back over my shoulder.

''No you didn't. Your mother has it.''

''Uhm, I mean my punch card.'' I turned and started toward the shed again. I thought of all the places I'd been after lunch. So much long grass. So much soft dirt. How was I ever going to find it? But I had to, before someone else did.

Then Maw called me. Maw's voice isn't something a person can ignore. Sighing, I stopped and turned around again.

Maw held my hat out the truck window. I could see my blue punch card sticking out of the bandanna I'd tied around the crown.

''Silly me,'' I said, hitting my forehead with the heel of my palm. I started walking toward the truck. How was I going to get out of this mess?

I shuddered as I bent, my back to the truck, and pretended to tie my shoelace. What I did, with trembling fingers, was reach around and grab a flat rock to pin into my pocket.

"Rosie Pearl," Maw called impatiently. "Right now! Or you'll walk back to camp."

Maybe after supper, I thought. But how could I come back to the fields, when Maggie was with me every minute of the day? I'd have to wait until night, when everyone was in bed. I'd have to go back alone.

I saw Maggie looking at me curiously. I flashed her a smile and patted the rock in my pocket. I'd never felt so rotten or deceitful in all my life!

I rushed through my supper, eating just enough to keep Maw from noticing how nervous I was. For once I couldn't wait for bedtime. If I was lucky, everyone would fall asleep before it got all the way dark. Then I could sneak back to the fields and look for the brooch.

But it didn't work out that way. Maw and Paw and Johnny Keats took their own sweet time eating. All I got out of eating fast was the chance to tote extra water when Maw noticed I was done.

When bedtime finally came, Johnny Keats kept us all awake by talking in his sleep. He does that when he's had too busy a day and too short a nap.

Anxiously I watched out the cabin door as the sky darkened. Our one little window doesn't let in enough breeze, so we leave the door open, too. Paw gets up during the night and closes it.

At last Maw and Johnny Keats were breathing deep and even and Paw was snoring up a storm. It still didn't look too dark out. Clothes in hand, I slid down from my bunk.

It seemed like at least a mile from my bunk to the door, though I knew I could cover it in two jumps when I was in a hurry to get to the outhouse. Tonight I was listening for creaky boards that might stop Paw's snoring.

On the porch I slipped quickly into my clothes and looked around. It seemed darker than it had from inside the cabin, maybe because out here I was alone. I started down between the rows of silent cabins, heading for the road.

A shadow rose from a porch and jumped down in front of me. I stifled a scream when a cold, wet nose touched my hand. It was Brandy, old Mr. Perez's dog.

"*Qué pasa?*" Mr. Perez called in his quavery voice. "*Brandy, ven tú aquí!*"

My heart pounded so hard I could hardly hear my own voice as I bent and whispered in Brandy's ear, "Get in there, you rascal, and don't never *ever* scare me like that again."

Brandy licked my chin, then jumped onto the porch and disappeared through the open cabin door.

I stood still for a minute, waiting for my heart to slow down. *Wish I could take Brandy with me,* I thought. *It's really dark now. My chances of finding that brooch tonight aren't all that good. Still, I have to try.*

I started off again, knowing I'd feel better once I got past the row of cabins nearest the road. Those cabins are kept for pickers who seldom stay in one place more than a week. The pickers who live in them are usually a rough lot.

I was just releasing the breath I had been holding when it happened. "What's your hurry, sis?" came a voice out of the darkness. "How about you stop and sit a spell?" The red tip of a cigarette glowed briefly, then arched through the night as the smoker flipped it away. I heard footsteps moving toward me.

I forgot all about Maggie's brooch. Turning, I sprinted for home. Deep, mocking laughter followed me.

When I got back to our row I was gasping for air. I wanted to run into the cabin, jump into my bunk, and cover up my head, like Johnny Keats does when I tease him about the bogeyman.

But my whole body twitched with fright. There was no way I could get into that cabin and up in my bunk without waking anybody.

I leaned against the porch post, ready to dash inside anyway if I heard more footsteps in the dark. "Take deep breaths," Paw always told me whenever I got scared or had the hiccups.

I breathed deeply now. The good and bad smells of a pickers' camp and a California summer's night mingled in my nose. I began crying. Tears of sorrow for losing Maggie's brooch. Tears of anger at her for talking me into carrying it. Tears of shame because she had trusted me.

A board creaked in our doorway. "Deep breaths, Rosebud," Paw said softly. "Till you can tell your paw what's wrong."

Chapter 11

I threw myself into Paw's arms and cried some more. When I was done, Paw reached into his nightshirt pocket for one of the soft, clean rags Maw keeps for wiping hot faces and blowing noses.

Then I told Paw what had happened to Maggie's brooch.

"Wait here," he said. He went back into the cabin, and I heard him talking to Maw. When he came back, he was dressed. He went to the truck and took out our lantern. "Looks like a fine night for a walk, Rosebud," he said. "Care to join me?"

Nobody spoke to us as we left the camp. Brandy must have been sound asleep on old Mr. Perez's bed. The cigarette smoker had disappeared. Sometimes when the camp is peaceful and quiet like that it's hard to believe some of the things that go on.

"Glad we didn't pick at Johanson's today," Paw said. "That's another hour away by foot."

"I'm sorry, Paw," I mumbled.

"I know, Rosebud," Paw said quickly. "I was trying to make

a joke." He reached over and ruffled my hair. It sure felt good being with Paw.

"Where do we start?" Paw asked when we reached the field. "Where's the last place you recollect having the brooch for sure?"

"At the shed," I said sadly. "If I hadn't been showing off to Shirley Jean, I'd never have lost it."

"What's done's done, Rosebud. But maybe we'll be lucky."

We searched the shed on our hands and knees. We did the same under the tree where I'd eaten lunch. Then we went out into the fields. We ran our fingers through the dirt until the lantern ran out of fuel. We weren't lucky; we didn't find Maggie's brooch.

It was past midnight when we started back to camp. By that time the lump in my throat was bigger than Maggie's lost brooch. I tried to swallow, but the lump wouldn't budge. "Oh, Paw," I wailed. "How can I tell Maggie that I've lost her inheritance?"

The moon lit our way down the road. Paw's face was troubled. "It's gotta be done," he said, giving my shoulder a squeeze. "Soon as folks know the brooch is missing, they can start keeping an eye out for it."

"But what if the person who finds it decides to keep it?"

"You won't be no worse off than you are now," Paw said. "But chances are just as good that whoever finds it will give it back."

"When do I have to tell her, Paw?"

"First thing in the morning, before we go to the fields."

When we got back to camp and I crawled into my bunk, I was sure I wouldn't sleep. What kind of person could sleep after losing her friend's inheritance?

But it had been a long day, even without the extra walk and

85

all the searching. The next time I opened my eyes it was morning and time to tell Maggie the awful news.

Paw went with me to the Campbells' cabin. Their door was open, and they were eating breakfast. Before I lost my nerve, I blurted out, "Maggie, I lost your brooch."

Maggie's eyes opened wide. Then she put her elbows on the table and covered her face with her hands.

I guess Mrs. Campbell didn't understand what I meant at first. But when she did, she gasped and jumped up, knocking over her stool. She dragged a wooden apple crate from under the bunk and pulled out a small carved box.

As she searched the contents of the box, I held my breath. Was I expecting a miracle? I knew the brooch wasn't in that box.

Mrs. Campbell lowered the box. She looked at her daughter, but Maggie didn't look back. Had Maggie taken the brooch without asking her mother?

"Margaret, how could you?" Mrs. Campbell whispered. Her voice rasped like a rusty pump handle on a winter day. She looked so sad I wanted to hide my face from her, too.

"Mother's brooch," she said. "I only wore it on my wedding day. Even then it wasn't mine. Mama was so set on it going to her granddaughter, because she had got it from her grandmother." She flipped her apron over her face and began to cry quietly.

For just the length of a hiccup I felt better. This was Maggie's fault. She shouldn't have taken the brooch without asking.

Maggie chose this time to look up at me. I saw the pain in her eyes. That's when I knew I never should have accepted the brooch, even for a day.

The silence in that tiny, hot room stretched on into tomorrow. Finally Paw cleared his throat. "We'll get the news out right away, Mrs. Campbell. There's a good chance the brooch'll be found and returned."

Mr. Campbell had stood up and was kneading his wife's shoulders. Her face still covered with her apron, Mrs. Campbell nodded.

"Well," Paw went on, "I guess we better get moving. See you folks at the truck when you're ready."

When we got to the pickers' shed, Mrs. Campbell hung up a piece of paper. She'd written about the brooch and asked folks to keep their eyes open for it. "I've got more of Margaret's old school papers somewhere," she said. "I'll make more notices after supper. The children can tack them up around the camp."

I supposed "the children" meant Maggie and me. But I didn't look at Maggie when her mother made that suggestion. I was pretty sure she wouldn't want me with her.

I didn't look at Maggie all that morning. And she didn't look at me. We both started off picking with our mothers. Everyone knows, when they see a kid my age picking with a parent, that kid is in trouble. But Maw kept up a line of chatter, and I made it through all right.

Still, everytime I went to the shed, there was someone reading that paper. Seeing it made me feel sad all over again. On the other hand, seeing so many people reading it cheered me up some and gave me hope.

That day we were picking peaches. My place was up on the ladder, handing the peaches to Maw. About midmorning Maw put me to picking with my sister, which meant I was up on the ladder again.

"If you wanna talk, I'm here to listen, Rosie Pearl," Lily Opal said. "But I'm not gonna force you. You might could use time to think it out first."

"Thanks" was all I trusted myself to say. My feelings were still too mixed up to make sense.

Between the quiet times, Lily Opal would talk about family matters. I was only half listening. Then she said, "I'm so proud of how you're growing up and learning to take responsibility, Rosie Pearl.''

My throat closed up tight. The tree I was picking from got all blurry. The peaches turned to fuzzy blobs. I swayed on the ladder.

It wasn't like Lily Opal to be so mean! She knew losing Maggie's brooch wasn't acting responsible. My eyes overflowed. Tears dripped from my chin.

Lily Opal gasped and stepped up on the bottom rung of the ladder. She pulled me down and hugged me close. ''Aw, honey,'' she murmured. ''I didn't think how that would sound to you right now. I was talking about the way you help Maw and look out for Johnny Keats.''

She pulled me down onto the grass. ''Listen close to what I'm saying,'' she said. ''I'm not looking to excuse you. Both you and Maggie are responsible for what happened to that brooch.''

''Only I'm the one who lost it,'' I wailed.

''Yes, but Maggie took it without her mother's say-so.''

''That's right,'' I said hopefully. ''If she hadn't taken it, I couldn't have lost it. She might be even more to blame than me.''

Lily Opal stared at me. ''No, she's not,'' she said firmly. ''And if you weren't so busy feeling sorry for yourself, you wouldn't ever have said that.''

''Hey!'' I squeaked. ''Whose side are you on?''

''Nobody's. I'm just trying to help you see that losing that brooch ain't all your fault.''

''I want to believe that,'' I said. ''But I'm pretty sure Maggie thinks it is.''

Lily Opal hugged my shoulders. ''You can't know for sure unless you talk to her. But you can't expect her to share the blame without accepting your part of it.''

I thought about that the rest of the morning. When lunch

break came, I knew what I needed to do. I was sitting under one of the shade trees when I saw Maggie come out of the shed. I got up and met her halfway.

"Maggie, I'm sorry," I said.

"Rosie Pearl, I'm sorry," she said at the very same moment.

"I've got more to say," I added.

She nodded. "Me too. But you go first, you're oldest."

"Maggie, I've done everything I can think of to find your brooch. If you know of something else, I'll try that, too."

Her face lit up. "Hey, Rosie Pearl, you didn't make one mistake in grammar that whole speech."

"Maggie!" I protested. "Quit fooling around. I'm trying to be serious."

Maggie's smile faded. "I know. And I'm trying not to. If I get serious, I'll start crying and blaming myself all over again."

"Blaming yourself?" I asked cautiously.

She grimaced. "Sure, it's obvious. If I hadn't made you carry the brooch, you never would have lost it." Her eyes filled with tears. "It's all my fault! Now what am I going to pass on to *my* granddaughter?" she howled.

I stood there for a second, too surprised to know what to do. Then I turned and yelled, "Lily Opal, you better get over here. We need you!"

With Lily Opal's help, Maggie and me agreed we were equally to blame. We spent the rest of the lunch break eating with one hand and searching the tall grass with the other.

When the break was over, we wanted to keep looking, but Paw said, "No, that brooch'll either turn up when we're least expecting it, or someone's already found it. If that's the case, we have to hope they'll give it back."

But nobody did.

We tacked up Mrs. Campbell's notices in all the field sheds and on every cabin row. We even hung them in the outhouses. And then every night after supper we asked from door to door if anyone had any news. Nobody did.

After a week we stopped going from cabin to cabin. Some folks still encouraged us. But others slammed the door in our faces. "People around here have enough problems of their own!" one man shouted. "Food on the table is a lot more important than a lost trinket." That made Maggie cry. We tried a couple more times, then stopped.

One evening after supper a bunch of us were over on the far side of camp, just sitting around under the trees, talking. It had been so hot that day, that was all we had the energy to do.

Maggie was teaching a younger girl to play cat's cradle. I was watching to see if she knew any new ways to do it that Lily Opal hadn't taught me.

Teddy was there, too. He'd been acting halfways decent since I'd lost the brooch. He'd even gone door to door with us and helped us put up the notices.

But I was really surprised when Betty Mae showed up, for the first time, with a couple of new girlfriends she'd made this summer. Betty Mae had avoided me and Teddy since that morning when I'd made a big thing out of Teddy picking her up on the rebound.

The new girls both looked to be older, about fifteen, but it was hard to tell, since they were wearing lots of makeup. I wondered if Betty Mae had given them some of her free Tangee lipstick samples. They were sitting a little ways from us, talking just to each other. I was really curious about why they were here. Every time I snuck a peek their way, at least one of them was looking at me.

The last time I peeked, Betty Mae was getting to her feet.

90

"Anyone want to play a kissing game?" she asked. She looked around the group and giggled.

A couple of other girls giggled. The boys shifted around nervously. I settled back and waited. Betty Mae was up to something.

"Bunch of babies," she said. Then she grinned and looked around again. "I know a game you guys might like." She glanced over at me. "Most of you, anyway. Rosie Pearl might be afraid to try it."

"That's all you know about it," I shot back, my dander rising. "You can't name a game I'm afraid to try."

Betty Mae moved closer. "It's called Truth or Dare."

I heard Maggie suck in her breath. "I thought so," she murmured.

I shot a quick look at Maggie. So she thought Betty Mae was up to something, too.

Several of the other kids started ragging at Betty Mae to tell them how to play the game. "We'll play," one said, "even if Rosie Pearl doesn't want to."

"Who says I don't want to?" I said. "How does it go?"

"Whoever is It," Betty Mae said, "gets to ask someone a question. That person either has to answer the question truthfully or take a dare." She smiled. "Simple, huh?"

"Just a minute," I said. "How do you know if they're telling the truth?"

"Oh, I thought of that," Betty Mae said quickly. She reached into the pocket of her overalls. I sucked breath when she pulled out a small black book. It was a Bible.

"Before we start," Betty Mae explained, "everyone has to swear on the Bible to tell the truth."

"No fair," Maggie protested. "Where I come from, we trust everyone's word that they're telling the truth."

Betty Mae snorted. "Well, mebbe that works where you come

91

from, but not here." She looked around. "Who else besides Maggie and Rosie Pearl is gonna back out?"

"Maggie and Rosie Pearl aren't going to back out," I said through clenched teeth. "We want to play."

"What do you mean, 'we'?" Maggie whispered.

I stared at her.

"Oh, all right," she said.

After that, nobody else backed out, either.

"How do you choose who's It?" I asked.

"I'm It," Betty Mae said, "because it was my idea."

"I knew it," Maggie whispered in my ear. "She is definitely up to something."

I didn't care what Maggie said. Betty Mae had thrown me a challenge. Us Bushes don't back away from challenges.

Betty Mae held the black book. She looked like a little kid who's just received an unexpected present. "Line up, everybody, and swear on this here Bible."

I got through that all right. Then Betty Mae had us sit in a circle. She got in the middle. As she turned slowly, looking at each one of us, some of the kids shivered or looked away. I wanted to tell them not to worry. I knew who she was going to choose. And why.

After a fine show of hemming and hawing, Betty Mae pointed at me. "Rosie Pearl, tell the truth, who do you want to marry when you grow up?"

"Uh-oh," Maggie said softly.

I cringed. *You and your big mouth, Rosie Pearl Bush,* I told myself. *You've done it again. And this time you swore on the Bible!*

When I looked around at the boys sprawled under the trees, most of them looked away. I didn't blame them. I didn't want to marry any of them, either.

When I got to Teddy, he bent and stared at his big toe. I'd been so mad at Teddy at the beginning of the summer, but he'd been real nice lately. Maybe he was coming to his senses, the way Maw had said he eventually would? Or was he just being nice so he could start saying he was my boyfriend again? Whether I named Teddy, or someone else, one of us was going to be embarrassed.

"Come on, Rosie Pearl," Betty Mae insisted. "Tell us who you like."

I shook my head. "I guess you're going to have to give me a dare, Betty Mae. I don't have an idea in the world whom I want to marry."

Betty Mae put her hands on her hips and stamped in the dust. But her eyes were shining gleefully. "I don't believe you, so I am going to give you a dare."

"No fair!" Maggie shouted. "She answered your question."

Betty Mae glared at Maggie. "You stay outta this, city girl. Everybody heard Rosie Pearl say she'd take a dare. And I'm gonna give her a real good one."

Maggie started to say something else.

I grabbed her arm. "It's okay, Maggie."

"Ready?" Betty Mae asked.

I nodded.

"Okay," she said. "I dare you to go into Jake Porter's bedroom and bring out something personal that belongs to him."

Chapter 12

"Something personal?" I squeaked. I couldn't believe even Betty Mae would come up with such a stupid idea. "From Jake Porter's bedroom?"

"Ah, fer pity sake," Betty Mae said. "'Tain't just his bedroom. It's where he lives. You know, back there behind his office? I s'pose he's got a bed in there, or somethin' to sleep on. Just bring me somethin' he wears or uses."

I sat there like I'd grown roots. I'd taken dares before. I'd even taken double dares. But Jake Porter's bedroom? All around me I could hear the other kids whispering and shuffling around.

When you go into someone else's house without their permission, you're trespassing. Not that anyone who lives in these camps has anything valuable. Maybe that's the point. All we have left is a need for a little bit of privacy.

But there's a word for taking something that doesn't belong to you. It's called stealing. I'd never stolen anything in my life.

Betty Mae shrugged. "Guess I shouldn't'a said bedroom." She tipped her head and grinned at me. "I've gone and scared you. Wanna call it off?"

That brought me up straight. Before that my ears had been buzzing. I'd thought maybe I was going to faint again. "Who's scared?" I demanded. "I'm not scared." But if I had to go through with this dare, and still stay out of trouble, I'd need to pay attention to what was going on.

"Then what are you waiting for?" Betty Mae asked with a familiar-looking smirk. "Go get something out of his, uhm, living quarters."

"But what?" I asked, stalling for time.

"I don't care," Betty Mae said impatiently. "Just something I'll know is his."

"But what if Jake's there?" I asked.

"He won't be," Betty Mae said firmly. "After supper he picked up my paw and a bunch of other men in that bus of his, and they went off to town to drink beer and play cards. They won't be back till late."

"Oh," I said again. "Well, what if the door is locked? Don't you suppose Jake locks the door when he goes off?"

"Of course he does, stupid," Betty Mae said. "But he hides the key in a tobacco can under the front step. You won't have any trouble getting in."

I stared at her, no doubt left in my mind that she had planned this whole thing ahead of time.

I started to say so, then noticed everyone was watching me. What could I say that wouldn't sound like I was weaseling out? I was sure this whole game thing had been a trap, but almost no one else saw it that way.

I needed time to think. There had to be a way to get out of this and still not seem like a coward.

"Where will you be while I'm inside?" I asked.

"What difference does that make?" Betty Mae hollered.

"Look here, Betty Mae," I said, "I'm not going anywhere or doing anything until I know exactly what I'm supposed to do, and where you'll be while I do it."

"It's like this, Rosie Pearl," Betty Mae said. "I've given you a dare, and you've accepted it. Now you have to bring me something from that back room."

"Okay," I said. "I can do that. But where will you be while I'm in there? Off telling someone what I'm doing?"

She rolled her eyes. "We'll be in the woods in back of the place. You can even choose someone to watch me, if you don't trust me."

"Trust you?" I burst out laughing. "Betty Mae, if someone trapped you into doing something as stupid as this, would you still trust them?"

She bit her lip. I guess she hadn't thought I was smart enough to see through her plan. Then she went back to looking mad. She'd been doing a pretty good job of keeping her temper. But I was doing better. I felt cool, calm, and in control.

"I'll keep an eye on her, Rosie Pearl," Maggie said.

"Me too," Teddy added.

Betty Mae's eyes flared at Teddy. "Thanks," I said. "But someone else can do that. You two are going with me."

"Hold on now," Betty Mae said. "Who said anyone could go in there with you?"

I shrugged. "No one, but no one said they couldn't, either."

I heard murmurs of agreement from the kids clustered around us.

"Don't worry," I said, as much for Maggie and Teddy's benefit as Betty Mae's. Maggie was staring at me like I'd gone crazy. Teddy was studying his big toe again. "They aren't going inside. They'll just watch and warn me in case somebody comes.''

''That's a relief,'' Teddy said. Maggie nodded.

Betty Mae rolled her eyes again. ''You're really taking all the fun out of this, Rosie Pearl. And besides, who put you in charge?''

''Sorry,'' I said. ''What happens next?''

''Well,'' she said confidently, ''you show me what you took, then you take it back.''

''Oh, no,'' I said. ''This is the first time you said anything about taking it back. After I bring it to you, the dare is over.''

Agreement from those gathered around us was loud and clear. ''But—but—'' Betty Mae stammered, ''what am I going to do with it?''

''Don't know,'' I said. ''And don't care.'' I stared at her. ''Want to call it off?''

She hesitated, twisting a button on her sweater until it came off in her hand. As she stuffed it in her pocket, one of her friends shouted, ''*No!* She don't want to call it off, do you, Betty Mae?''

Betty Mae was having a real hard time. She couldn't seem to look at me, so she looked at her friends. They crossed their arms across their chests and stared her down. ''No, I don't wanna call it off,'' Betty Mae said, glaring at me. ''It's not like we was gonna keep whatever you bring out.'' She shrugged and looked back at her friends. ''Heck, if she's scared to put it back, we'll do it, won't we?''

I almost laughed out loud. Those two girls had turned as white as ghosts under all their makeup. '' 'We'?'' one of them choked.

Betty Mae sighed deeply. ''Okay, I'll put it back. I never intended for anybody to really steal anything.''

I was relieved. If Betty Mae put back whatever I took, then it

97

wouldn't be stealing. But could I trust her? I felt scared and alone. *Oh, please, God,* I prayed silently. *Please don't let me get caught. I'll never do another bad thing in my life; just don't let me get caught.*

It didn't take us long to get to Jake Porter's shack. It was just the other side of the woods. And I didn't have to choose anyone to watch Betty Mae. All the kids came with us. They didn't want to miss anything.

Sure enough, when we got to the edge of the woods and looked out, Jake Porter's bus was gone.

I looked off toward the mountains. The bottom of the sun was a couple of inches above them. It was going to be dark soon. ''Why don't you guys wait—'' I started, then stopped at a look from Betty Mae.

''We'll wait here,'' she said in a hoarse whisper.

''Come on,'' I said to Maggie and Teddy. We circled the edge of the clearing, staying in the woods as long as we could. Maggie and Teddy went and hid in the bushes where they could watch the road.

Then I took a run for the front door. I stopped at the bottom of the steps and looked at the door. The padlock was in place and shut. I fell to my knees and looked for the tobacco can under the bottom step.

I grabbed the key and hit that porch at full speed. My hand trembled as I fumbled to fit the key into the padlock. It popped open with a loud snap. I was now past the place where this whole thing was Betty Mae's dumb idea.

I laid the padlock and the key down on the porch. The door creaked slightly as I opened it and peered inside. It was getting darker by the second.

Beyond Jake's desk was the doorway to the back room. No one I knew had been back there since Jake Porter had been hired as job boss. I looked inside. They hadn't missed much. That room was a mess. A rickety old kitchen table stood in the middle of the room. A bare lightbulb hung from the ceiling over it. An old newspaper, spotted with grease, lay crumpled next to a chipped mug and an empty pork-and-beans can. The handle of a spoon stuck out of the can. I curled my lip, remembering Maw saying, "Only hoboes and folks who are trash eat right out of the can."

Under the window, beyond the table, a chipped sink over-flowed with dirty dishes. A fly buzzed and bumped against the glass, trying to get out. The place stunk worse than a whole pile of dead skunks!

Fading light from the window fell on a cot, its blankets trailing on the floor. Next to the cot was a low dresser. Hanging over the edge of the dresser was Jake Porter's tie. That was something Betty Mae would recognize. Jake wore that tie every day.

I hurried toward the dresser. As I dragged the tie toward me, something under it scraped across the top of the dresser and fell to the floor. I saw it just before it rolled under the dresser. It was red, and it was round, and it looked a lot like Maggie's brooch!

Chapter 13

I was down on my hands and knees, groping under Jake Porter's dresser, when Maggie came running across the office. "Rosie Pearl," she gasped from the doorway. "Did you find anything yet? There's a car or a truck coming down the main road. Teddy says we should get out of here."

My fingers had found what they were searching for, but I still wasn't positive that it was Maggie's brooch. Instead of looking at it, I jumped up and followed her out of the shack, slipping it into my pocket. Jake Porter's tie trailed from my hand. It felt cold and greasy. I held it up as I ran. "Yeah, I found this."

We pulled the front door shut behind us. I picked up the padlock, threaded it through the hasp, and clicked it shut. Then I threw the key into the tobacco can, shoved the can under the porch, and we took off for the woods. As we crouched behind a thick bush, I reached into my pocket and fingered the round object. It sure felt like Maggie's brooch. Suddenly Teddy was there.

"That truck kept on going," he said. "Did you get what you went after?"

I held up the tie again. "Yes, I did." As I pulled my hand out of my pocket I said, "Actually, I think I got more than I went after."

When I opened my hand, Maggie gasped.

"Lord Almighty," Teddy said. "Where did you find it?"

Maggie had taken the brooch from my hand and was holding it against her cheek. Tears slipped through her fingers and over the bright stones.

"On Jake Porter's dresser," I said. *Now who's a thief?* I wondered.

Teddy looked thoughtful. "We can't keep it, you know."

"What are you talking about?" I asked. "It's Maggie's, isn't it?"

Maggie's eyes got real big. She clutched the brooch so hard her knuckles turned white.

Teddy nodded. "Sure, it's Maggie's brooch. But if we take it now, who's gonna believe where you found it?"

Teddy was right. The only way we could put the blame on Jake Porter was for the brooch to be found by somebody else where I had found it, in Jake's shack.

"But Teddy," I said, breath suddenly real scarce in my body. "That means I have to go put it back. And then I have to go get someone and bring them here to find it. How am I going to explain why I was in there in the first place?"

Teddy smiled. "Not you, Rosie Pearl, *we*. *We've* got to put it back, then *we've* got to bring someone here to find it. And *we* have to think up a pretty good explanation of how we came to find it."

He grabbed me with one hand and Maggie with the other. "C'mon, let's go."

101

"Wait a minute," I protested. "First I have to go show this tie to Betty Mae."

Teddy frowned. "That's really gonna slow us down, and it's gettin' late!"

Maggie was still clutching her brooch and looking back and forth between us.

"I'll take care of Betty Mae," I said, taking off for the part of the woods where the gang of kids waited.

"Oh, gosh, oh, golly," Teddy rattled on, pulling Maggie along with him. "We could be in for a lot of trouble."

We burst through into the clearing. There didn't seem to be so many kids now. I shoved the tie under Betty Mae's nose. "Recognize this?" I demanded. "You should. I think it's the only tie Jake Porter owns."

Betty Mae wrinkled her nose. "It's his awright. The dare is over, Rosie Pearl." She thrust out her hand. "Hand over the tie then."

I shook my head. "Not necessary. I've decided I don't need anyone to finish things for me." I waggled my finger at her. "You stay right here," I ordered. "If we're lucky, maybe all of us can come out of this without any trouble."

"Come on," I said to Teddy and Maggie. The three of us took off again through the woods. There was still no one at the shack. "You stand guard, Teddy," I said. "Maggie is coming with me this time."

Maggie still hadn't said anything except an occasional "No, no," but she followed me willingly. Once again I unlocked the padlock and laid it next to the key on the porch.

I pulled Maggie across the office and into the back room. I pointed to the top of the dresser. "The brooch was right there, Maggie. Under the tie. You put it back, and I'll put the tie on top of it."

"No, no," Maggie whispered. "I'm not going to lose it again."

"Maggie," I said softly. "If we don't leave your brooch here now, no one will ever know that Jake Porter found it and kept it."

"Ooooh," Maggie moaned, sounding just like her maw when she'd found out the brooch was lost. Slowly she reached out and put the brooch on the dresser. I draped the tie over it, and we left. But this time, after I clicked the padlock shut, I hid the key under a rock behind the shack.

When the three of us got back into the woods, Betty Mae said, "Did you remember to put the key back in the same place?"

"What a question," I said, crossing my fingers behind my back.

She glared at me for a moment, then turned and stomped off toward camp.

"Show's over," I told the few hangers-on. "Let's all head for home."

"So," I said to Teddy and Maggie, "who are we going to tell, and what's our story?"

Surprisingly, it was Maggie who answered. "First thing we're going to do is go get Teddy's baseball and throw it through Jake Porter's window."

"What?" Teddy shouted. "Are you crazy?"

"No!" I shouted back. "She's a genius!" I grabbed Maggie and hugged her. "An absolute genius."

Teddy was still sputtering and questioning Maggie's sanity.

"It's the perfect excuse for going into Jake's cabin," I insisted.

"But what if Jake keeps my ball?" Teddy asked.

"He's not going to keep it. We'll throw it through the window, then go right in and get it. We'll show it to whoever we tell about the broken window, then say we went in to get the ball and spotted Maggie's brooch."

"But who's gonna pay for the broken window?" Teddy muttered.

"We'll worry about that later," I said.

Teddy still wasn't fully convinced that Maggie's idea would work, but when we got to his cabin he went in and got the ball anyway.

We hurried back through the twilight woods. "Who's gonna throw it?" Teddy asked. I shrugged. "It's your ball," I said. He nodded.

When we got to Jake's for the third time, Teddy stood in the middle of the clearing in front of the shack. I couldn't watch. I knew how special that ball was to Teddy. His brother had left it for him the night he'd gone off with Walter Scott.

I raced around the shack to get the key. Just as I picked it up, I heard the crash.

"Good for you, Teddy Tate," I whispered. "Good for you."

I put the key back in the tobacco can under the front step after we got the ball.

"Who shall we tell?" Teddy asked when we were halfway to camp.

"Well," Maggie said, breaking her long silence, "since we're all in this together, we'll each tell our own father. They can decide what to do."

I winked at Teddy. "Didn't I tell you she was a genius?"

That was a long night. First our paws got together and talked to each other, then they talked to us. And then we all got sent to bed! I didn't go to sleep for a long time. I was so mad not to be in on the ending.

At breakfast the next morning Paw told how the night before

the three fathers had got into our truck and driven to Mr. Northrup's. They'd used the Northrups' phone to call the sheriff. When the sheriff came with a warrant, they all drove to Jake Porter's place.

Jake arrived at the same time they did. He wasn't too happy to see the sheriff, or our three fathers, or Mr. Northrup. He was even less happy when he saw the warrant.

Of course he denied having heard anything about the brooch being lost, but nobody believed him. Unfortunately, nobody could prove he had heard about it. Mr. Northrup said the growers were going to let Jake Porter go at the end of the season anyway, so he fired him on the spot.

"Mr. Northrup told Jake to be packed up and out of here by morning," Paw finished. "So that's the last of Jake Porter. He's gone, and he'll soon be forgotten."

But Paw was wrong for once. Jake might be gone, but he wasn't going to be forgotten for a long time. When we went out to climb in the truck that morning, all four of our tires had been slashed. Mr. Campbell ran to look at his car. Jake Porter had struck there, too. But only one of Mr. Campbell's tires was slashed, and not nearly as bad as on our truck. He'd be able to patch it.

Something must have scared Jake off before he finished off the Campbells' tires and got to the Tates'. Theirs were untouched.

Lots of folks had to walk to the field that day; there was only so much room in other folks' vehicles. Jake, of course, had taken off with his rickety old bus.

There were some mighty glum faces in our three families that day. "If I'd had to buy new tires for our car, it would have taken all my savings for getting back to my uncle's farm," Mr. Campbell told Paw. "How are you going to replace yours?"

"I don't know," Paw said softly. "I guess we'll all have to work a little harder."

I felt so bad about those tires. I knew I was going to be working my hardest.

That day notices went up in all the field sheds that the Valley Growers' Association would be interviewing for a new job boss. About every man I knew signed up for a chance at that job, and some boys, too.

Chapter 14

Maw and Paw were both so glad that Jake Porter was gone, their hearts just weren't in it when they frowned at me for being anywhere near his cabin. Maggie and Teddy said it was just the same with their folks. In fact, the whole camp was celebrating Jake's absence.

I knew Paw had a pretty good chance of getting the job. He knew Mr. Northrup so well from doing extra jobs for him. But I didn't know how good his chances were until the night Mr. Northrup showed up at our cabin.

Maggie and I were sitting on the porch after supper when he came driving up. As he strode up onto the porch, he said, "Good evening, ladies, solved any more crimes lately?" We giggled. "Your folks at home, Rosie Pearl?" he asked.

"Yes sir," I replied. "They're in there drinking coffee with Maggie's folks, Buddy and Lily Opal, and Robbie Burns and Mavis." He nodded and went on into our cabin. A few seconds later I heard Maw shriek.

I ran into the cabin, and there she stood, her apron tossed up over her face, just like Mrs. Campbell had done when I'd lost Maggie's brooch.

"What happened?" I shouted.

Paw and Mr. Northrup chuckled. "I've just given your father some good news, Rosie Pearl. He's our new job boss. I guess it came as a big surprise to your mother. I don't know why. Your father was the number one choice of all the growers."

I looked back at Maw. She was still standing there, and her apron was shaking. "What's the matter, Maw?" I demanded. "Aren't you happy? Isn't this the best thing that's happened to our family since we lost the farm?"

Slowly Maw lowered her apron. Most everyone was looking at her with open mouths. But Paw had a silly grin on his face. "Course she's happy," he said. "That's just her way of showing it."

"Well," I said firmly, "I don't think that's any way for a pregnant woman to act!"

Maw almost tossed her apron over her face again. "It ain't right for you to say such things, Rosie Pearl."

"How come?" I asked. "Everyone knows you're going to have a baby. Women who are going to have babies are pregnant."

"Good for you, Rosie Pearl," Maggie whispered from the doorway.

"Children are growing up too fast these days," Maw said, shaking her head. "But Orrin's right. I'm happy as can be. I ain't had this much to be happy about for a long time now."

Maw got out another cup for Mr. Northrup, and everyone sat back down again. As they were getting settled, Maggie leaned her chin on my shoulder and started asking questions. "Are you going to keep on picking, now that your father is job boss? Are you going to move out of camp?"

Mr. Northrup grinned up at us, then turned back to the grown-ups. "Jake's old place will be too small for the four, I mean, five of you. So the growers have agreed to buy the old Watkins place. It's been empty for several years and will need some fixing up."

Paw nodded. "I can do that."

Mr. Northrup smiled. "I know you can, Orrin. And the growers will get together the materials you need. You'll probably want to stay here while you work on it."

I was relieved to hear we wouldn't be living in Jake's old place. I didn't think even Maw's scrubbing could get it to smell good.

"I can give you an hour or two in the evening after supper, Orrin," Mr. Campbell said. "If it weren't for you, I wouldn't have this job."

"Buddy and me will help, too, Paw," Robbie Burns said.

Well, that answered one of Maggie's questions. I was just as curious as she was to find out about the other one. But I didn't get a chance. More people were stepping up on our porch and sticking their heads in the door. Like I said, news spreads fast in a migrant camp.

Paw and Mr. Northrup stepped out onto the porch. There must have been a dozen people gathering out there, talking and speculating. After Mr. Northrup told them the news, offers for help came in as fast as folks could make themselves heard.

I was sure there must be more than one man who was disappointed not to get the job, but nobody said so. Everyone nodded in agreement when one man said, "It's gonna be a heap more pleasant around here with you as job boss, Orrin."

For more than an hour the people kept coming. The men shook hands with Paw, the women smiled at Maw, some with just a touch of envy in their eyes, I thought. But my maw's not one to put on airs. Without even taking off her apron, she sat down on the edge of the porch and visited with everyone who came by.

"You're a good woman, Edith Bush," one of the women said. "The Valley Growers' Association is getting double its money's worth by hiring your husband."

I should have known better than to think that just because my paw was now job boss I wouldn't be picking anymore. The growers got together used tires for the truck, so after that Paw would drop us wherever we were picking that day, then drive around to all the fields to see if there were enough pickers. If there weren't, he had to go into town and see who he could round up. But if there were, he could go work on our house.

Our house! It had been a long time since I had said those words. The Watkins place, which was fast becoming called the Bush place, had just two bedrooms. I would have to share a room with Johnny Keats. But that was sure an improvement over all four of us in one room.

At the end of each day, Paw came back to the fields to pick us up. Other than that, not much changed for a couple of weeks.

Then late one August night, Buddy came pounding on our front door. "It's Lily Opal," he gasped when Paw opened the door. "She's having terrible pains."

"Oh, no." Maw groaned. "She's got six more weeks to go."

Paw pulled on his trousers over his nightshirt, but Maw just grabbed a quilt and threw it around her. Checking to see that Johnny Keats was still asleep, I followed them out of our cabin and into Lily Opal's.

My legs felt like cooked spaghetti as I leaned against the table and watched Paw kneel down by my sister's bunk. "What's the matter, honey?" he murmured.

Lily Opal raised her head from the pillow. Her face was shiny

110

with sweat, and her eyes stared like they weren't seeing anything. But she heard Paw's voice.

"Oh, Paw," she gasped. "It's my baby! My baby's coming and it ain't time yet." She fell back onto the pillow. I grabbed the table when she cried out from the pain.

"Rosie Pearl," Paw said. "Get Ed Campbell and Robbie Burns in here right quick."

"I'm here, Paw," Robbie Burns said from the doorway. "I'll get Mr. Campbell."

"And back your truck up to the porch, Son," Paw said. "I'll need you and Ed and Buddy to help carry her out there."

Paw stood up. "I'll get dressed whilst you get her ready for traveling, Edith. She's going to the hospital."

Maw choked back a sob. Then she grabbed a clean nightgown from the line over the stove and, with Buddy's help, put it on Lily Opal. She tucked the coverlet tight around my big sister, just the way she had wrapped Johnny Keats when he was a tiny baby.

"She's ready, Orrin," Maw said as Paw strode back into the cabin.

The four men each took one corner of the mattress tick. They carried Lily Opal out the door and put her into the back of the truck in one smooth motion. Maw had her own clothes in her hands when she climbed in after Lily Opal.

Paw gestured at Robbie Burns. "You drive. Maw and Buddy and me will ride back here with your sister. And mind the ruts!"

"Yes, Paw." Robbie Burns jumped into the cab of the truck and started the engine.

"What about me, Paw?" I asked.

"Stay with your little brother," he said.

Maggie and her mother came and stood by me. Mavis was there, too, holding Johnny Keats. She had caught him up as he stumbled sleepily out our door, looking for us. I watched the truck until it turned the corner onto the highway. And I kept on watching long after it was out of sight.

Mavis touched my shoulder. "Come along, Rosie Pearl," she said quietly. "I'll help you take your brother back to bed. If you need me, just holler."

"Good Gosh Almighty," Johnny Keats squealed, bold with his words since neither Maw nor Paw could hear him. "How come ever'body was making such a ruckus? You woke me up!"

I swung around, the fear I'd been holding in exploding into anger. My open hand was aimed right for Johnny Keats's face. Mavis stepped back and turned away from me. My hand hit her on the shoulder.

"Rosie Pearl!" my little brother shouted indignantly. "What'd you wanna go and hit Mavis for?"

"It's all right, Rosie Pearl," Mavis said. "It's all right."

But it wasn't all right. Babies weren't supposed to come a whole month and a half early. And it wasn't right that I had wanted to hit my brother. I ran into our cabin, slammed the door, and threw myself on Paw's bunk. I buried my face in his pillow and began to cry. My sister, my Lily Opal, her baby . . .

Chapter 15

The sound of the truck engine woke me up. It took me a while, lying there on Paw's bunk, to figure out why I wasn't up in my own bunk. Then there was a knock on a nearby door, and I heard Mr. Campbell say, "Just a minute, I'm coming."

"Sorry to bother you again," came Paw's voice. "We need help getting Lily Opal into her cabin."

Lily Opal! I ran to the door and stepped quietly onto the porch.

Mr. Campbell came along our porch, shrugging his suspenders up onto his shoulders. "Was it false labor, Orrin?"

Paw shook his head. "No, she's worse off than when we left."

"Oh, no!" I cried.

Paw came over and hugged me. "You scoot on back to bed now, Rosebud. Your maw will be in to check on you soon's we get Lily Opal settled." He glanced toward our door. "How's Johnny Keats?"

I hesitated. I hadn't thought once of my little brother since I'd tried to smack him and then stormed off to cry on Paw's bed.

"The boy is fine," Mr. Campbell said quickly. "Mavis put him back to bed."

Gratefully I slipped back into our cabin. Sure enough, Johnny Keats was asleep in his bunk.

Later, when Maw came in, I was sitting at the table. "Rosie Pearl!" she exclaimed. "Why ain't you in bed?"

"I'm waiting to hear about Lily Opal, Maw. I've been worried."

Maw sighed. "Of course you have, poor child." She sat down across from me and laid her head down on her arms on the table. "And the worst ain't over yet."

"Tell me what's happening, Maw," I begged. "If Lily Opal is worse, how come she isn't in the hospital?"

"They wouldn't take her in," Maw said.

"But why not?" I asked. "Couldn't they see how bad off she was?"

"They could see," Maw said sadly. "But we didn't have no money. That's a private hospital. They don't let folks like us in without you put down fifty dollars."

"But couldn't you borrow the money?"

"We tried," Maw said. "We told them we could get the fifty dollars and more, if needed, from Mr. Northrup."

She sighed again. "But the Northrups wasn't to home. We begged the folks at the hospital to take Lily Opal in and we'd go for the money. They kept saying no, not without money."

"But Maw, there has to be a hospital somewhere that takes folks without money."

Maw nodded. "Yes, the county hospital. But it's another thirty miles away. We didn't have no money left for more gas.

114

And even if we got some, it was too far for her to go in her condition."

"Maw," I whispered, creeping around the table and into her arms. "Is Lily Opal going to die?"

Maw held me close. "No, no," she crooned. "Nothing of the sort. Your sister's gonna be just fine."

Buddy poked his head in our doorway. "I've started a fire in our stove and Lily Opal's bed's all ready," he said. "She'll want you right there when we carry her in." Buddy could hardly hold his head up, he was so tuckered out.

"Back to bed, Rosie Pearl," Maw said, giving me a little shove. She got up slowly. "I'll be sitting with Lily Opal as long as she needs me." I knew better than to argue with that tone of voice. "But I'm just next door if *you* need me," Maw added.

I woke to find sun streaming across the floor and Johnny Keats tugging at my shirt. "Mrs. Campbell says you're to come next door for breakfast!" he shouted.

"Tell her I'll be right there," I mumbled as he ran back out the door. I tumbled wearily out of bed, splashed cold water on my face, and ran my fingers through my hair.

Then I peeked out the door. I would go to the Campbells' for breakfast all right. But first I was going to see my sister!

I looked to the left, then to the right. No one in sight. I tiptoed to Lily Opal's door. Taking the knob gently in my hand, I turned it. When I heard the click of the latch, I pushed the door open. Buddy and Lily Opal were in their bunks. Paw was in the rocking chair, and Maw was on a pallet on the floor close to Lily Opal. They were all asleep.

On a low stool next to Maw stood a cardboard box with a blanket over it. The box looked like a miniature of the covered wagons I'd seen once in a history book, except that out one end hung an electric cord. A faint light glowed through the blanket.

As I stood there trying to figure out what to do, I heard what sounded like Tabby's newborn kittens. I used to follow that sound when I searched for the place she'd hidden them in the barn back home.

I poked my head into the box. Lying on its side was the tiniest baby I'd ever seen. Its back was to the heat and glare of the lightbulb. All that showed was its face and the one wrinkled fist it had worked loose from the wrappings. I touched the baby's palm, and the tiny fingers flew wide, then slowly came to rest on my finger, light as a butterfly.

"Hello," I whispered. "I'm your Aunt Rosie Pearl."

The tiny mouth moved, as if to answer me. Then the hand flew away from my finger and the baby gasped, again and again. The pale blue veins in its forehead disappeared as the doll-like face turned red.

"Maw!" I screamed. "Maw, wake up. The baby's choking."

Maw turned over and scooped that baby up in one motion. She pressed her ear to its chest and motioned us to be quiet.

Lily Opal was trying to get out of bed. "Buddy, set by your wife and calm her," Maw ordered. "Orrin, build up that fire and get the kettle to boiling. This little mite's got congestion in her lungs."

A girl! Lily Opal had a daughter and I had a niece. Then I looked at my sister, and my joy popped like a soap bubble. Her mouth was open in a silent scream.

I backed into a corner and sat on the floor. Scared as I was, I wasn't about to be sent out again.

Mrs. Campbell looked in the door. "Edith, can I help?"

"I need a tight-wove blanket for a croup tent, Nellie," Maw said. "Can you spare one?"

With a nod, Mrs. Campbell disappeared, then reappeared in less than a minute with the blanket. Paw took an edge, and they draped the blanket from the hood of the stove and down over the steaming kettle.

"Orrin," Maw said, crawling under the blanket with the baby, "this may just help temporary. See if you can find Mr. Northrup and ask him, if need be, can he go back to the hospital with us. This time we've got to have money."

The baby had one more coughing spell before Paw and Mr. Northrup got there. It was worse than the first but didn't last as long.

Maw was sitting in the rocking chair now. When I looked at Maw in the chair and the baby in the box on her lap, my throat tightened. Would Lily Opal ever get to sit in that chair with her baby?

"Mrs. Bush!" Mr. Northrup exclaimed as he came in. "I'm sorry I wasn't around when you folks needed me last night. But I've got money with me now. Enough for whatever's needed." He peered into the cardboard box at the baby. "How early was she?"

"Six weeks," Buddy answered. "Do you think she'll make it, Mr. Northrup?"

"I don't know about such things, Buddy. But Doc Stewart will. I called him before I came here. He's gonna call the hospital about an incubator. He should be here soon."

"A doctor?" Lily Opal asked weakly. "We can't pay no doctor. We can't pay no hospital, neither." She raised herself up on one elbow. "I tried to tell that to Paw last night, but he wouldn't listen."

"Well, you listen to me now, Mrs. Brown," Mr. Northrup said firmly. "You're not to worry about such things."

I had to smile at the meek way Lily Opal laid back down. She wasn't used to anyone but Maw or Paw talking to her that way.

*　*　*

When Doc Stewart arrived, he bustled right in and took charge. "What happened at that hospital?" he demanded, after examining first the baby and then Lily Opal.

"Humph!" he snorted when Paw told about being turned away from the hospital because they had no money. "These are hard, hard times," he said sadly. "But that doesn't make it right. No sirree," he went on, slapping his hand on the table to emphasize each word, "That *still doesn't make it right*!"

He pursed his lips thoughtfully. "You're just as well off here," he told Lily Opal. "But we'll take your baby back to the hospital. They've got an incubator, and I'll see to it that they take good care of her."

Lily Opal tried to sit up again. "Maw," she pleaded. "Oh, please, Maw, don't let them take my baby away."

"Now, Mrs. Brown," Doc Stewart said, his voice as firm as Mr. Northrup's had been earlier. "Your baby doesn't have much of a chance to live without an incubator. Your mother has done a fine job with her up to now, but her lungs are very congested."

Lily Opal turned her face to the wall and began to cry in great, gulping sobs.

"I'll be going along with our little girl," Buddy said. The doctor nodded.

I walked quietly over to the bunk and sat down. "Don't cry, Little Sis," I whispered. "Everything's going to be all right now. Isn't that so, Doc?" I looked up at the doctor hopefully.

He frowned. "I'll do everything I can, but don't get your hopes too high." He shook his head. "I'll do my best for your little girl, Mrs. Brown," he said, but he didn't look at Lily Opal when he spoke.

Then he turned and said briskly, "Let's go, folks."

Mavis stayed to look after Lily Opal and Johnny Keats while

118

Maw went with Buddy and the doctor and the baby. Paw and Mr. and Mrs. Campbell took me and Maggie to the fields.

"Best thing we can do is keep ourselves busy," Paw said.

Trouble was, my hands were used to picking without me thinking about them at all. That left my mind to think about anything it pleased. All morning long I remembered the soft touch of those tiny fingers.

Maggie tried her best to get me thinking about other things. "I can't *not* think about her," I said finally. "I wish you'd seen her, too. Then maybe you'd know how I feel. It's as if she'll only be real as long as I keep on thinking she is."

Maggie nodded. "Okay, if that's what you need, then tell me every little thing you remember."

"There's not an awful lot to tell," I said. "I only saw her face and one hand."

"Tell me about her face."

"Tiny," I said. "Her mouth is so small, I'm sure they'll have to use a dolly bottle to feed her. We did that once, when Sheba had more pups than nipples."

Maggie giggled. "Oooo, Rosie Pearl, you said *nipples*!"

That got a little smile out of me. Maggie looked pleased.

"Her nose doesn't look hardly big enough to breathe out of," I went on. "But the most amazing part is her eyebrows. You can't see them at all unless the light is right."

"And her eyes?" Maggie prompted. "What color are her eyes?"

"I don't know," I said slowly.

"It's okay," Maggie said quickly. "Nothing to feel bad about. They say all babies' eyes look blue when they're first born anyway."

"But she never saw me!" I cried. "She's real to me because I saw her. But I'm not real to her. She didn't see me!"

Then I just couldn't help it; I sat down at the bottom of that peach tree and had myself another real good cry. Had it only been one night since Lily Opal had gone to the hospital and been turned away?

I looked up a couple of times to see how Maggie was getting along without me. I could tell she was thinking hard about something from the frown on her face.

All of a sudden she came down the ladder and plunked down her basket. "Think about this, Rosie Pearl," she said, shaking her finger at me. "That baby wouldn't have seen you clearly even if she had opened her eyes. But she held on to your finger. It's just as easy to tell what's real by feeling as it is by seeing."

She put her hands on her hips and glared down at me. "That baby knows you're real all right. Now start picking! I'm way ahead of you."

Maw and Buddy came back just before suppertime. They had taken a bus all the way back to camp. Mrs. Campbell made Maw sit down in the rocking chair before she would let her talk. Then she went back to her own cabin to finish up making supper for all of us.

"Doc Stewart's staying overnight," Maw said. "He'll call Mr. Northrup to pass on word to us if there's any changes."

"How was she doing when you left, Maw?" I asked.

"She was in a real incubator and breathing good."

Buddy nodded. "She did look better, honey," he told Lily Opal.

"When will we know if . . . ?" Lily Opal's voice was weak.

Buddy sat gingerly on the edge of the bunk and held her hand. "Doc says if she makes it through the next couple of nights, she'll likely make it all the way."

"Such a little girl to be all by her lonesome in that big hospital," Lily Opal said.

"I know, honey," Buddy said. Then he smiled. "But them nurses is so sweet with her. I told them not to go spoiling her, though. I said my wife wouldn't take kindly to that."

Buddy got a little smile out of his wife, just the way Maggie had done with me.

After supper we waited on the porch until after dark to see if Mr. Northrup would come with any news, but he didn't. "That's good," Maw announced, getting up to take Johnny Keats in to bed. "Means she ain't no worse."

The rest of us didn't set there long after that, partly because folks kept coming to ask about the baby. It was nice of them to ask, but I could tell it was getting harder and harder for Paw and Buddy to answer them.

I wasn't surprised when everyone turned in early.

Next day Maw stayed with Lily Opal and the rest of us went to the fields. I was having a hard time understanding how grown-ups could go on picking and cooking and other ordinary things as if nothing unusual had happened.

I studied their faces as we worked. Most of the time there was nothing to see but a blank face and empty eyes. But if anyone caught me looking at them, they'd smile, then turn away. I kept my questions to myself.

Chapter 16

Mr. Northrup came by that evening. "Don't be alarmed, folks," he said quickly. "Doc says there's no change and after tonight maybe you can start to breathe a little easier."

Again we went to bed early, even though the next day was Sunday and we could sleep in.

It was close to morning, though not full daylight yet, when I heard Paw get up to answer a soft knock at the door.

"I'm sorry, Orrin," I heard Doc Stewart whisper when Paw opened the door. "I did all I could to keep her, but she just slipped away."

Paw stood there, outlined by the rising sun.

"Do you want me to go with you to tell the parents?" Doc asked.

Paw nodded. "I'll get my trousers on." He shut the door.

"Was that Doc Stewart I heard, Orrin?" Maw asked quietly. She swung her feet to the floor. "Has something happened to the baby?"

Paw stood in front of Maw, his hands on her shoulders. I heard him take a deep breath before he spoke. "She's gone, Edith. We have to go tell our daughter and her man that their baby girl has died."

Maw moaned—an awful, sorrow-filled sound—and reached for her wrapper. I didn't try to follow Maw and Paw; they'd have just sent me back. *But if I can hear what's happening, I'll feel better,* I thought. I pressed my ear against the wall. I was wrong.

Lily Opal's scream and her husband's curse were followed by a window-shaking bang as something crashed against the wall. I found out later it was Lily Opal's rocking chair. Then there was silence.

I buried my face in my pillow and began to beat on it. *I'm mad!* I shouted inside my head. *Mad at that hospital for not taking in Lily Opal in time to save her baby's life. And I'm mad at this depression for making Buddy and Paw be migrants with no money for a hospital.*

I sat up and sucked my bruised fists. "It's not fair," I whispered. "I never even got to hold her."

There was a service for the baby that evening, in front of our cabin row, so Lily Opal could hear it. She hadn't wanted a service, and even after Buddy and the doctor convinced her, she begged them to leave the door shut.

"Mrs. Brown," Doc Stewart said. "There has to be a time for saying good-bye, even to a little one you've only had for two days." He reached down and squeezed her hand. "You don't believe me now, but a service will help."

By the time evening came and lots of folks had gathered, I started to understand how Lily Opal felt about wanting to be left alone. The anger inside me was such a private thing. Why couldn't we all be left alone so our hurt could go away?

I sat on the edge of the porch right outside our door. Maggie sat with me. So did Teddy Tate.

Teddy didn't say a word when he sat down. He just gave me a little smile and an awkward pat on the shoulder.

There was a banjo and a fiddle and a guitar for the hymn singing. Mr. Tate had once been a lay preacher, so he read from the Bible.

" 'To everything there is a season, and a time to every purpose under heaven: a time to be born, and a time to die . . . a time to weep, and a time to laugh; a time to mourn, and a time to dance . . .' "

I couldn't see how it would ever again feel like a time to dance in our family.

As if he had read my mind, Mr. Tate said, "Some of you might be havin' a bit of trouble understandin' what this verse means."

You're right there, preacher, I thought.

"This here's the way I see it," he went on. "There's a right and proper time to weep and mourn. That time is now for the family of the baby girl most of us never even got to see. But that time can't go on forever.

"Soon it'll be time to stop mournin' and get on with livin'. Some of us ain't gonna feel like laughin' and dancin' right away, but if we hold on to weepin' and mournin' too long, we may forget how to get back to livin'."

He raised his long, skinny arms. "Let us pray."

All through the prayer I wondered about what Mr. Tate had said. How would I know when it was time to stop weeping and get back to living? When I thought about the days ahead, I couldn't imagine myself ever laughing and dancing again.

Maw and Paw and Buddy had stayed with Lily Opal during the service, but after the amen, Paw and Buddy came out to thank folks for coming.

There were lots of folks there, most because they had known our family for some time. Some just came from curiosity or the hope there would be something to eat. That lot disappeared right fast when no food was set out.

Maw stood at the cabin door, talking to folks. "Just leave your condolences with me," she said. "I'll pass them on to Lily Opal. She ain't well enough to have visitors yet."

I went and sat way back in the dark inside our cabin after Maggie and Teddy left. I felt a little better and wondered why. Had the doctor been right about the service helping to say good-bye? Or was it what Mr. Tate had said about taking time to weep and mourn before getting back to living?

"I'm sorry for the Browns," I heard a woman say. "It's hard to lose a first child."

"But the family's bearin' up right well," another replied.

"A mite too well, if you ask me," came the response. "I've been watching Orrin. It don't seem natural to me for a man not to grieve when his first grandchild dies."

"I reckon yer right."

"Of course I am. Mark my words, Orrin Bush ain't gonna be himself again until he lets himself mourn."

I got up and started for the door, my anger rising like a swarm of bees. Who did those busybodies think they were, gossiping about how my paw should act? I'd tell them a thing or two!

But Maw was just next door with Lily Opal. What if she heard me?

Shaking and close to crying, I sat back down. *What do other people know about what is and isn't natural for my paw? Don't they know what a strong man he is? Strong men don't cry.*

But that wasn't true. Summer before last when Teddy's maw died, Mr. Tate cried. Right out in the open where anyone could see him. Mr. Tate was every bit as strong as Paw.

Paw was mourning, wasn't he? Just because nobody had seen

him cry didn't mean he wasn't taking his time to weep and mourn.

It was my own fault for listening in on people. I had to listen when Maw and Paw told Lily Opal and Buddy that their baby had died, and I was sorry for listening.

I had to sit there in the shadows and listen to what folks passing by said about the service, too, and now I was sorry about that.

I shook my head angrily. So what if it was my fault for listening in on people? Nobody had a right to say my paw wasn't acting natural.

The next morning Mr. Northrup took Maw and Paw and Buddy into town for a private burial service in the town cemetery. Mavis stayed with Lily Opal and Johnny Keats again. And the rest of us? What else? We went to the fields to pick.

After lunch Maw and Paw and Buddy showed up in their work clothes and started picking. That seemed to be the end of that. But it wasn't.

Chapter 17

First of all, Paw became so quiet I was never quite sure he knew what was going on around him. Just the same, he got up each morning, went to the fields, and worked a full day. Every evening after supper he worked for several more hours on our house.

"Don't pester your paw," Maw warned me when I tried to talk to him. "He's awful tired from working all day and in the evening, too."

But it was more than that. I really missed our special times together. Paw had always liked a back rub when he was extra tired. Now if I touched his shoulders he shrugged my hands away with an apologetic grin.

Then there was Lily Opal. She should have been up and around the next week, but she wasn't. She didn't go to the fields or cook a meal for Buddy.

"At least come and sit under the trees whilst we pick," Maw urged her. "The fresh air will do you good."

But Lily Opal only shook her head and turned to face the wall.

Finally, one evening at suppertime, Maw set Paw's plate in front of him and said, "Orrin, something's got to be done about Lily Opal."

Paw looked up and frowned. "What did you say, Edith?"

Maw sighed. "I said, something's got to be done about Lily Opal."

Paw looked confused. "I thought Doc Stewart said she was fine now."

Maw nodded. "He did. But if she's fine, why is she still laying in bed all day?"

Paw waved his hand as if brushing away a fly and began to eat his supper. "Don't be hounding the girl, Edith," he said between bites. "She'll get up when she gets bored with being in bed."

"I don't think so," Maw said. "I think she needs a talking-to. And I think you're the one needs to give it to her."

"Lord Almighty!" Paw shouted. He threw down his fork and jumped to his feet, knocking his stool over. "Ain't it enough I work all day and half the night? Do I have to start doing the doctoring, too?" He began to pace around the crowded room.

I started to get up, startled and frightened by this new side of Paw. Maw threw me a quick look of caution, and I settled back.

Johnny Keats reached for my hand and started to whimper. "Shush now," I whispered. "It's gonna be all right." I hoped I was right.

Paw picked up his stool and slammed it back onto its feet. "She's got a husband, Edith," he said in a hard voice. "Let him talk to her."

"He tried," Maw said quietly. "Buddy ain't been a husband but a short time. He don't know what to do when Lily Opal won't answer him."

128

Paw stopped pacing. "Well, *I* do," he said, and he stomped out the door.

Johnny Keats and I stared at Maw, wide-eyed. There was a little satisfied smile on her face.

"Maw," I protested. "You shouldn't have riled Paw up like that. He's liable to say things he doesn't mean."

Maw sat down at the table and picked up her fork. "I don't think so, Rosie Pearl."

"Lily Opal Bush Brown!" we heard Paw roar. "I want to know what's going on around here!"

"What do you mean?" we heard Buddy ask.

"You get yourself next door, Buddy," Paw ordered. "One of us ought to sit down and eat a hot supper tonight, and it don't look like it's gonna be me."

We heard five quick steps; then a wild-eyed Buddy burst in our door. Maw stood up. "Set yourself down, Buddy," she said as if nothing unusual was happening. "I'll fix you a plate."

He sat down, but raised up a bit when Paw started hollering again.

"You hear me, Lily Opal? I said turn around and look at me. I've got something to say to you."

After a short silence we heard, "That's better. Now listen here, daughter. The time for mourning is over! Your maw and the doctor say it's time you were up and taking care of yourself and your man. And I say so, too."

Another little patch of silence followed. Then all of us lifted from our stools when Paw hollered, "What's that you said?"

This time we had no trouble hearing Lily Opal. Her voice came through the wall every bit as loud as Paw's. "I said," she hollered right back at him, "who are you, telling me it's time to stop my mourning? You ain't even started yours yet, and that baby was your grandchild!"

129

"Awwww," Maw groaned. Buddy jumped up to comfort her, but she motioned him back. "He'll be all right now," she choked out. "They'll both be all right."

I wasn't all that sure. It was awful quiet next door.

Maw got up, and we followed her out onto the porch. Robbie Burns and Mavis were already there. Maw beckoned them to follow us.

I'll be a forgetful old granny before I disremember my paw sitting in that rocking chair with its patched-up arm, holding my big sister in his arms and rocking her back and forth. Tears poured down Paw's cheeks. Lily Opal was dabbing at them with a faded rag.

Paw's face, in fact his whole body, seemed to soften and relax as he cried out his sorrow. Lily Opal's face was snuggled into his neck as she held him.

That's when I swore a promise to myself that nobody in my family would ever again be kept from having help because we were migrants.

I'm not sure yet how I'm going to keep that promise. Part of it, I suppose, will be to wait out this depression. And part of it will be to get better schooling than I have the past few years. Whatever it takes, that's what I'm going to do.

I may never wear lace on my underwear or taffeta bows in my hair. Maybe Maw and Paw will never own a house or land of their own again. My brothers may always work for someone else. But what happened to Lily Opal isn't ever going to happen to one of us again.

I know, at last, that what Mr. Northrup said about our family is the truth. There is no telling what we all will go on to do or be, once this depression is over.

Epilogue, 1940

That wasn't the last time any of us cried, when we remembered the baby that died.

But now, four years later, Paw has started buying and planting land of our own—just an acre at a time, but it's a start. Buddy has taken over as job boss for the Valley Growers' Association.

We finally heard from my brother Walter Scott. He and Teddy Tate's brother had got into a lot of trouble and spent some time in jail. When they got out, Walter Scott joined the Civilian Conservation Corps, then got himself a year-round job on a ranch up North. The Tates haven't heard from their son.

Robbie Burns and Mavis moved North to work with Walter Scott. The rancher Walter Scott was working for was getting ready to retire, but he wanted to stay on the land, so Walter needed more help. Their boss is an old bachelor, and he's worked out an agreement with my brothers to buy his land from him, while they work there.

Maw's last baby was the girl she'd hoped for. She was born at the county hospital. Maw named her Florabunda Emerald. We call her Flory Em. She keeps Maw real busy, now Johnny Keats and I go to school full-time. She's almost four, and big enough to have her nose out of joint over Robert Service Brown, Buddy and Lily Opal's new baby boy.

Robert Service was born at the county hospital, too. It's not as grand as the hospital that wouldn't take Lily Opal in, but it's a real step up from being born in a tent like Johnny Keats.

Teddy Tate and I have remained just friends. He still wants to be a farmer someday. But as for me, there are just too many sad memories connected with working the land.

I'm halfway through high school, the oldest one in my class, because of all the school I missed. But, as I would have said before Maggie taught me better: That don't make me no never mind! My teachers say if my grades stay as good as they've been, I can apply for a college scholarship. In spite of the depression, some private organizations are still offering scholarships, even to folks like me. Whether or not I get one, I'm determined to go to college. I may have to wait out more than the depression before I go, but I'll go. There's a war threatening in Europe. President Roosevelt promises to keep us out of it, but I wonder if he can.

Well, that's about all there is to tell. Except Maggie and I still keep in touch, through letters. They're still living back East on Mr. Campbell's uncle's farm. Times have been kind of tough for them, too, but Maggie says life there is easier than migranting.

We hope to see each other again, someday, maybe after college. I haven't decided yet what I'll be, but Maggie says she thinks she'll surprise her mother and be a teacher. After all, she did a pretty good job with me!

AFTERWORD

*H*istory books call it the Great Depression and claim it started October 24, 1929, when the stock market crashed. But for many farmers like Rosie Pearl's father, the depression started earlier in the 1920s.

Farmers had not yet learned that uprooting all the prairie grass would lead to soil erosion. Or that planting the same crops in their fields every year would wear out the soil. As each year's crop used up more nutrients, the crops got poorer and poorer. So did the farmers. They couldn't grow everything they needed. Things they had to buy, like flour, sugar, and shoes, as well as parts for farm equipment, were very expensive. But every year the money farmers received when it came time to sell their crops dwindled. There was seldom money left to buy the next year's seed.

Farmers went to the banks and mortgaged their lands, homes, livestock, and equipment. Sometimes they even borrowed money against the next year's crop.

Then came the droughts. In his book *Growing Up in the Great Depression,* Richard Wormser wrote, "From sunrise to sunset, the skies were clear blue from one end of the horizon to the other. The weather was a picnicker's dream, but a farmer's nightmare. For blue skies meant another day without rain, and without rain there would be no crops."

The droughts continued for almost ten years. Temperatures reached 121 degrees Fahrenheit in some states. But the worst was yet to come. Huge windstorms came and blew away the cracked and lifeless topsoil. America's Wheat Belt became the Dust Bowl.

Now there was nothing to plant and nowhere to plant it. No seed, no soil, no rain, no crops. Banks took away and resold seven hundred fifty thousand farms. Nearly four million farm families left the land. Four hundred thousand of them headed for California.

Four hundred thousand new people competing for jobs in a state already jammed with people out of work! No wonder the Bush family was anxious to get on the road that year.

Life was extremely hard for migrant workers. Many camps were little better than the Hoovervilles Maggie described to Rosie Pearl. Disease, drunkenness, and abuse were common. Working hours were long, from sunup to sundown, or as one migrant described it, "from can't see to can't see." Wages ranged from fifty cents to a dollar a day.

Pickers' cabins were crowded and always in need of repair. Most camp owners left repairs to the residents, not even supplying materials or tools, much less labor.

What little electricity there was often failed. Water pipes broke and water became polluted. Repairs were done or not done, depending on the attitude of the camp owners.

It was this attitude that made the Bush family's choice of one particular camp understandable. Though there were men like Jake Porter who sought to make themselves feel more important by making the pickers feel less so, there were also men like Mr. Northrup: camp owners and crop growers who, though they had hardships of their own, sought to treat their workers with dignity.

And there were families like the Bushes and the Campbells, who responded to that treatment and kept working for better days. Without hiding the bad parts of migrant life, I have tried to show the strength of those families.

The depression was a time of great contrasts. As a small child growing up in the city, I got sick of canned tomato soup for lunch every day. It cost ten cents a can. But a friend of later years, who had lived on a farm during the depression, said, "We never had money to buy canned soup. But we had a garden. I got sick of fresh tomato soup!"

I complained about going to school with cardboard covering the holes in my shoes. My friend replied, "We went barefoot to school, unless there was snow on the ground."

Talk to your grandparents, or older adults, about the depression. You may hear of hard times that broke families apart. But maybe you'll hear stories of hard times that made families stronger. Families like yours and Maggie's and Rosie Pearl's.

ABOUT THE AUTHOR

Patricia A. Cochrane, a native of Seattle, began her college career when her youngest child entered first grade. Twelve years later she graduated from Seattle Pacific University with her first grandchild in the audience. Then she began her next career, writing for children. Patricia Cochrane and her husband have three grown children and three grandchildren. *Purely Rosie Pearl* is her first novel.